To Cousin Rachel,
may you enjoy reading
and be inspired to life a
life of good choices.
Hubert S.

Divinely Constructed
Humanly Lived

HUBERT SCHMUCKER

Special acknowledgments are due to the collaborative work of Steve Oyer (SO Photographic, LLC); to Virginia Leichty for her brutally honest editing input; and Eyedart Creative Studio the book design. Their expertise helped give the book a greater chance of success.

This book is a work classified by the author as neo-fiction. While there could be a correlation between real-life scenarios and events, equal liberties were taken to disguise the characters, places, and times to protect the innocent or guilty. Therefore, names are fictitious, locations are nebulous, and titles are modified, allowing the reader's imagination.

Reference to the Evangelical Free Church in no way intends to demean, declare or define the actual doctrine, polity, or government of that Church. It is simply the author's reference to an entity he respects as a viable Christian Church.

Published by LeePen Media Expressions, Goshen, IN

Table of Contents

Preface

Writing, for some, is an expression of creative thinking. For others, it is a catharsis of built-up emotions. And a few attempt to record a memory for the benefit of their readers. This author's motivation is a little of each of these.

Having just completed the first publication of a historical narrative entitled Family Preserves, the writer decided to attempt a second foray into penmanship. Is this success going to his head, a lapse in reality, or perhaps stupidity?

Family Preserves received many comments and notes of appreciation from family and friends. Readers enjoyed the information and style. Kathleen asked several times when she could expect a second book.

The reader will become quickly aware that this author likes to use an abundance of analogies. And equally prominent is the insertion of puns and attempt at humor through colloquial words and phrases. Hopefully, the reader will not get lost in this writing style but will find it amusing.

For whatever reason, here goes another try with hopes that it will be both entertaining and contemplative. After all, life has both its exhilarating and sobering moments.

Can life be categorized into symmetrical increments? For the main character in this story, decade markers appear to imply its feasibility. The author includes in each period: 1) A building metaphor; 2) Predominate family dynamic; 3) A key life focus; 4) Relatable biblical references.

The above segments maintain no rigid order. Variety has always been the preference of this writer's thoughts and practices. It's easier than breaking a habit. And hopefully will be more interesting for the reader.

At the same time, life is not static. Frequent challenges and crises come to test one's character and moral resolve. Each is obligated to consider the consequences of choices made in life. It is this process that becomes the subject of this story.

Happy Trails, H.L.S.

Introduction

The stage was set two weeks earlier. The natural cycle provided the perfect internal environment for the imminent miracle. A loving attraction led to the height of passion, and the race had begun; a human race.

On this hot August night, 250 million genetic "soldiers" swam vigorously to be the first to find and merge his DNA with an equally genetic complete egg. A cleverly devised turn onto "fallopian way" allowed one to outmaneuver 400 others who had survived the trip. BONANZA! He found the prize and staked his claim. The miracle of conception(C) was complete in hours. Life had begun.

As he (medically termed a zygote) floated downward into mom's uterine wall, this single-celled entity divided rapidly into hundreds of matching DNA cells. The winning sperm carried the "Y" chromosome, predestining it to be male. The transformation he would experience in the next thirty-seven weeks(W) is truly a divine miracle.

At C+2W, he was now an embryo about the size of a poppy seed. His residence was a perfect incubator providing protection and nourishment for continuing multiplication of cells. These cells had the blueprint for determining every body part's shape and function.

"Hey, what's that sound?" asked the embryo. "What's that moving through my body?"

At just C+3W, a beating heart circulated blood throughout his tadpole-shaped body. In a week, he had expanded to a sesame seed's size. He realized that he had his swimming pool of amniotic fluid for comfort and development.

Though the parents were oblivious to his existence, something told mom that things were not the same. A trip to the doctor revealed the news that a baby was on the way! Mom's dream of building a family was coming true.

Within C+4W, nose, mouth, and ears took shape, and during the following week, he doubled in size. Now paddle-like forms extended at the end of arms and legs. A slight movement began in week six. Nails appeared on fingers and toes by the end of week eight. At the end of the first trimester (C+12W), fingerprints had developed, brain cells were firing, functioning organs were visible through his translucent skin, and he could suck his thumb.

At C+14W, mom may feel her baby's kick, and morning sickness may come. The baby might detect bright light through mom's stomach wall and his closed eyelids. Now the baby's gender might be detectable by sonar imaging.

The five senses allow the baby to hear voices outside the womb at C+17W, and at C+21W, he can differentiate speaker's voices. Ironically he has grown to become the size of an ear of corn. It's too late to tell him not to drink the pool water. To develop his lungs further, he inhales and exhales amniotic fluid around C+24W.

By week twenty-five, the baby establishes a sleep pattern. Mom wishes it were the same as hers. Usually, there is no hiding her expanding abdomen. And baby's movements can be felt by Dad and others as his activity increases.

The pace is quickening. The final trimester of pregnancy can be grueling. Baby only knows it's time to kick it up a notch. Starting C+30W weight gains are about one pound a week. By C+34W, he is the honeydew melon's size, so weight gains decrease to an ounce a day. Now the lungs and other organs are in final development.

During weeks thirty-six and thirty-seven, the baby shifts to be head down, Mom's bone structure modifies, and soon indications come that it is TIME. Labor pangs intensify, and she takes her position on the delivery table.

On May 11, 1948, an eight-pound twenty-one-inch (3.63kg/533.4mm) boy made his appearance amid the groans of a mother and the first cries of a child. What an incredible nine-month journey. What a prelude for the road ahead.

"For you created my inmost being; you knit me together in my mother's womb. I praise you because I am fearfully and wonderfully made; your works are wonderful, I know that full well." Psalm 139:13-14

NOTE: Credit for the intro information goes to Baby Center in their online article, "Fetal Development Week by Week" by Kate Marple/Medically reviewed by Judith Venuti, Ph.D., Embryologist/May 22, 2019. The number of weeks listed in the introduction shows two weeks less than those listed by the Baby Center article. The Baby Center's report begins two weeks before conception, while this writer starts at impregnation.

CHAPTER 1

Footer

"Train a child in the way he should go, and when he is old he will not turn from it." Proverbs 22:6

Cedric Allen Myer was birthed on a Tuesday at 6:05 PM in a hospital in the Midwest state of Indiana. His parents were lower-middle-class people with a strong work ethic. Cedric's mother acquired a nursing degree while his father was a self-taught vehicle mechanic who operated a repair shop and eventually set up a used car sales business.

Cedric was quite active. He enjoyed kicking his legs and began crawling in the ninth month. Initial non-aided steps came one week after his first birthday. He was generally well-behaved and had a gentle personality.

He considered eating an eager venture. His mother nursed him through the fifth month before switching to bottle feeding. Perhaps he enjoyed it so much because she would sing lullabies, children's Bible choruses, and other calming songs. Cedric's favorites were "Jesus Loves Me," "Rockabye Baby," and "He's Got the Whole World In His Hands." Her music resonated with Cedric since he heard it pre-birth. Her clutching arms also brought comfort and reassurance of her love. She was an accomplished singer and practiced with her family.

Father's after-work home arrival became a highly anticipated time. It meant getting swung into the air and wrestled on the floor.

"Catch," dad would say as he threw a ball to Cedric.

They both liked time together when available.

As always, parents long to hear their child's first words. Cedric cooed and babbled at three months. He listened to their urging to identify them, and at six months, Father won.

"Da-da" became his first recognizable word.

"Ma-ma" followed three months later.

Pets were a regular part of the family. Grandma Miller gave Cedric a rabbit on his first birthday. At age two, five puppies were born, and Cedric loved to hug them, almost to the point of choking. He enjoyed numerous toys, especially a truck that he cherished selfishly. Games of all varieties became play and educational tools.

He developed relationships with other children quickly. His cousins, school, and church brought many opportunities to broaden his friendship circle. Cedric often made requests for visitors to be guests at his home.

The addition of siblings radically changed family dynamics. Five months after Cedric's second birthday, a sister named Dorinda was born. Sixteen months later, Rowena, another sister, came along. Fortunately for Mother, another three years passed before fraternal twins Willis and Willow became part of the Myer household.

Between her children's births, Mother reduced her work hours to two nights per week. Dad's schedule allowed him to be available at home as needed. And the older siblings shared in doing chores as they matured.

It necessitated the expanding family to move to a larger house. A four-bedroom, two-story house with a barn and three acres in the same area became the ideal purchase. It provided the space to play and raise garden produce.

Cedric had learned to occupy himself by the time Dorinda arrived. He was curious if this new person who dominated Mom's time was good or bad. Holding her was a privilege until she started crying or soiled her pants. Cedric realized he had a new playmate when she grew old enough. All this was great till she began getting into his things.

"Dori's taking my truck," he would yell, or, "I don't want her to eat my Cheerios."

Cedric was generous to a point, but there were limits. As Dorinda turned three, she was less of a pest. Plus, they both had an interest in Rowena, the new kid on the block. Now they needed to be a team to protect their property from a new threat.

By the time Cedric turned six, the three sibs developed into buddies. He would take his sisters on wagon rides to see the rabbits behind the barn. On occasion, they became mischievous. Once, they found Mom and Dad's secret box in their closet and found letters and a gun inside. They knew it was off-limits to them. As he reached for the gun, Dorinda grabbed the muzzle, and it fired. Dorinda screamed in agony with blood squirting from her hand.

"Mom, mom," Cedric yelled.

"What did you do?"

"The gun hurt Dori."

Mother rushed Dorinda to the hospital with the help of neighbors. The result was the loss of two fingers on her left hand. Remorse filled Cedric's heart, and guilt became heavy for many years, being reminded by Dori's disfigured hand. It was the last time he touched a gun for the rest of his life.

Early on, the parents taught the Myer children the tenants of God's Word. Truthfulness, love, kindness, and obedience were essential to observe. The regular attendance in Sunday School and worship affirmed these values.

Having a spiritual footer was stressed as necessary, but academic education was also for one's formidable advancement in life. Grades one through four provided Cedric with the basics to build on. He liked to learn and had teachers that encouraged him to pursue his interests.

Elementary years provided Cedric with numerous friends. Boys and girls both were easy to communicate with, and he found none to be antagonistic. His closest friend was Bob, who liked to play softball, watch westerns and operate model trains. This friendship meant less time spent with his sisters, but it provided a broader community base.

Willis and Willow's birth came near the end of Cedric's first grade. Willis had brown hair and brown eyes, weighing six pounds-five ounces, and was nineteen inches long. Willow was longer (twenty-two inches) and heavier (seven pounds-two ounces). Her hair was blond, and her eyes were blue.

Dorinda and Rowena did their best to be mommy's helpers caring for the twins. Feeding them formula and later baby food items were their joy. Holding them was delightful while asleep, but playing with them on the floor was better still.

Cedric loved each of the twins but was drawn more to Willis being the same gender. Seven years difference created fewer common interests and activities with them. Willis, however, idolized his brother.

The first decade was a good foundation builder. Family and friends enabled Cedric to practice the heart's virtues and broaden his worldview. However, his curiosity and trusting nature opened him to disappointments and hurt that became difficult to overcome.

CHAPTER 2

Walls

"Be happy, young man, while you are young, and let your heart give you joy in the days of your youth. Follow the ways of your heart and whatever your eyes see, but know that for all these things, God will bring you to judgment." Ecclesiastes 11:9

A house's walls set parameters, give structural integrity, and create barriers to outside elements. Choices made in youthful times are critical in building character and determining adulthood directions. Many factors influence the decisions one makes. Consequences will always follow the choices made.

For Cedric, the years from ten through twelve were relatively carefree and joyful. Many decisions were made for him by his parents and teachers. Life went well if he followed household rules, completed his studies, and showed up for meals. He was very compliant and obedient to those in authority over him. However, there was a need for discipline on occasion.

Cedric recalls hitting Dorinda when she took pens out of his backpack. His Father took exception and returned the favor with a couple of whacks on his behind.

The worst part was having to say "sorry" to Dorinda when he didn't mean it.

Dorinda stuck out her tongue at him and whispered, "You better hide them good because I'll find them and retake them."

Another incident occurred near age twelve when staying overnight with his friend, Bob.

"Let's go to the feed mill and see if some other guys are there," said Bob.

"Yeah," said Cedric, "maybe we can have a corn cob fight with them."

The mill had closed for the day, and sure enough, several area boys were present. Everyone collected loose cobs on the ground and took cover behind wagons and the building. The battle was on. Some shots hit their target, but most missed by a mile.

As Cedric aimed at Kenny, the cob flew high and broke a window. There was an instant scattering of boys not wanting to take the blame. As Cedric left with Bob, guilt flooded over his conscience.

"I think we need to go back in the morning and tell the owners what happened," said Cedric.

"We could be in big trouble," noted Bob, "and what will your dad say?"

"He'll say, you're going to make it right, "replied Cedric.

That night was long and sleepless as Cedric contemplated the confrontation. In the morning, Bob and Cedric walked back to the mill and found Cappy, the owner.

Cedric spoke, "Some of us guys were here last night to have a cob fight." He admitted, "I threw one, and it broke the window. I will pay for a new windowpane," promised Cedric.

"Well, you might as well stick around," Cappy retorted, "the police are on their way."

Now fear came over the boys as they considered the consequences. A policeman came and talked first to Cappy. Then he approached Cedric and Bob with a frown.

"You mind telling me what happened?" he asked gruffly.

"A bunch of us boys had a cob fight last night, and one of mine broke the window," Cedric confessed. "I told Cappy I would pay to have it replaced."

"Well, you may have more troubles to face," the policeman stated, "seems that somebody has been dropping stones in the grain cars at the railroad." Then he added, "You could be facing some charges of delinquency."

The boys explained that neither had been near the train cars nor had put stones in them. After the policeman conferred with Cappy and spoke with Cedric's Father, he told the boys they must not set foot on the mill property in the future. Ironically, about three years later, Cedric was hired by an area farmer and delivered some grain for him to that mill. The owner did not make an issue with him.

Cedric was not adverse to work. At age ten, he took on a small paper route. Work brought the reward of having money to purchase various items at the local market. Occasionally, he would stop at dad's shop and help with odd jobs like cleaning or stocking products. In the mid-teen years, additional tasks became available, producing more significant compensation and provided Father and son the opportunity to work together and for Cedric to learn a trade.

Rowena and Dorinda became envious of Cedric's riches. They frequently asked for money to satisfy their worldly desires.

When that failed to work, Dorinda would hold her left hand in front of his face as if to say, "You owe me."

He was reluctant to empty his pockets but was generous, and at times purchased them treats. His guilt was persuasive.

It became Cedric's duty to mow the yard. A riding mower quickened the chore. An elderly neighbor lady struggled to keep up with her mowing.

"Would you allow me to mow your lawn? I'll do it for free" "

"That's very kind of you but I'll give you five dollars," insisted Mrs. Cripe.

It resulted in two other neighbors hiring Cedric to mow their lawns and paid him ten dollars each. Of course, dad asked him to assume the cost of gas.

By age thirteen, changes were occurring. Cedric began showing evidence of puberty. The twins had slept in the same room since birth. Now Willis was moved into Cedric's bedroom. It thrilled Willis but was quite an adjustment for Cedric. He lost his privacy, and Willis was not as neat, plus he snored.

The Myer girls also saw modifications. Rowena and Willow shared a bedroom, giving Dorinda a private one. Perhaps it was best for this maturing young lady who liked to stay up late reading or doing artwork.

Now that the twins were six, Mother picked up three days of work per week. Her absence placed more responsibilities on the older girls preparing meals and doing laundry duties. Willis took over the care of the rabbits, chickens, and pets. Everyone shared part of the load running a house.

At this time, Dad set up his used car sales. His lot allowed for about ten to twelve vehicles. He preferred specializing in GM products, but an occasional Ford or Chrysler would sneak onto the lot.

The summer of Cedric's fourteenth birthday was between Junior and Senior high school. He gave up his paper route and spent more time at Dad's shop filling gas tanks, checking the oil in cars, and washing their windshields. His father also taught him how to change the oil and filters in vehicles. Three dollars an hour wasn't "chump change" in that era.

Increased work brought limited time for extra-curricular involvement. Sports and clubs at school and playtime with Bob became less of an option. However, the church youth activities provided many social and spiritual resources. It offered vacation Bible School, youth camps, and weekly Sunday School. Most important was the moral teaching and Christian modeling by the adult mentors. The pastor's sermons were practical and inspiring.

Cedric invited Bob to join him for the youth programs. It gave them both alternatives to questionable peer activities. The fast pitch softball league was of particular interest for a sporting outlet.

All these factors led Cedric to commit himself to choose Christ as his personal Savior and Lord in the fifteenth year of his life. But a nagging struggle with the lack of assurance that this decision was enough to get to heaven plagued him for several decades. Faith had not finished its work in Cedric's heart.

Cedric maintained a B-Plus GPA through high school. He excelled most in math, history, and accounting. Credit goes to having such encouraging teachers in these subjects.

A crucial goal as a teen was to operate a car. Completion of Drivers Education took place in the summer of Cedric's fifteenth year. The law then allowed him to drive when a parent sat in the seat beside him. But in June of his sixteenth year, he was given a legal license by the BMV.

Father had been looking for an appropriate vehicle for Cedric. Though not his first choice, Cedric purchased a 1949 Mercury sedan. It was sleek black and had a V-8 engine with an overdrive. It lacked in "chick appeal" but made up in speed. It could "haul."

Cedric, though not a stud, was a romanticist speaking of chicks. He knew the impact of flowers, jewelry, and poetic cards on a girl. His first crush was Ellen, around age seven. His first gift to a female interest was an eighth-grade classmate named Dorcas. However, his first date wasn't until age seventeen.

His first date was a disaster with Pam. She didn't like the movie they saw or the restaurant's food. He dropped her off at her house by letting her get out of the car independently. There was no second date with her.

Trish was a more successful date at first. They went to a drive-in restaurant followed by a swim at the lake. Their second outing a month later was to the 4-H fair. But after the third venture, a Christian concert, Trish declined any future invitations.

Striking out twice, Cedric was hesitant to try again for a while. The following Spring, Bob asked him to consider going on a blind date with Carma. Bob's girlfriend Monica was a classmate of Carma. A double date was set for the four to go to a dinner and movie.

Bob and Cedric picked up the girls at Monica's house. Upon arrival, the guys got out of the car, and Cedric opened the door for Carma. Entering on the opposite side, he wasn't sure how close to sit, so he hugged the door.

Carma was petite with blond hair and hazel-colored eyes. She was wearing a beautiful red and white striped skirt with a white blouse. Around her neck was a silver chained cross. Her lipstick was candy apple red. If Carma planned these first impressions, she hit a home run.

Conversations to Chucks Barbecue were immediately free and easy.

"Hi Carma, I'm Cedric."

"Hi Cedric, I've been looking forward to this evening."

"What school do you attend?"

"I'm a junior at Central High. And you?"

"I attend Bacon Hill and am a junior also."

"Tell me about your family," Carma asked.

"I'm the oldest with three sisters and a younger brother."

The questions continued related to hobbies, home locations, work, and food preferences. The thirty-minute trip seemed short. And they had the whole evening ahead.

They ate dinner with light-hearted talk and laughter. The girls ordered smaller portioned items while the guys chose regular-sized ones. Each was careful not to drip barbecue sauce on their clothes. From there, they went ten blocks to a theatre showing "The Sound of Music."

"Would you eat some popcorn if I purchased it?" asked Cedric

"Maybe a little."

"What about a drink?"

"I'll have a diet coke, please," replied Carma

"Would you prefer a separate bag of popcorn?"

"No, I'll share with you."

The movie was fantastic with well-performed musical numbers. The storyline was dramatic yet full of romance. Cedric felt Carma's hand, and they interlocked fingers as the scene of Maria and the Captain danced in the pavilion.

Talk about getting a charge. The rest of the evening was exhilarating. The four arrived back at Monica's house around 11 PM.

Cedric walked Carma to the door, thanked her for a grand evening, and asked, "May I call you next week?"

"I will look forward to that," she said.

Cedric and Carma dated approximately in two-week intervals the rest of their Junior year. On his birthday in May, Cedric asked Carma if she would accept his class ring to indicate a steady relationship. Her answer was to slip hers off and traded with him. They sealed it with a kiss; it was their first.

One's senior year is often the best. Usually, with required classes completed, it allows one to choose electives. Guys may try taking Home Economics, or choir and three study halls. They desire to get their diploma and be out of school.

Cedric managed to sign up for two accounting classes to go along with Business Introduction and Civics. All of these were forenoon classes enabling him to arrange an afternoon careers track working at Dad's shop. It benefited them both.

When cleaning, Cedric discovered a box of explicit men's magazines in the shop's closet. They caused a mix of curious fascination and questionable moral conflict regarding his dad's presumed behavior. The pictures became etched in his brain.

Father planned to entice Cedric to work full-time for him after graduation. Between graduation and retirement was adequate time to train his son. He failed to discuss these goals with Cedric.

Mother hoped her children would all enter a college or trade school. Her attaining a nursing degree was a monumental feat with non-supportive parents and a lack of finances. But she remained determined and focused on her goals.

"I want you children to obtain all the education you need to succeed," she said.

"I want to be a mechanic just like dad," Willis replied.

Cedric still wasn't sure of a career pursuit. Dorinda was bent on being an artisan in either wood sculpting or painting; she was good at both. Rowena spent hours perusing fashion and travel magazines and dreamed of faraway places. The twins were approaching their teens and not totally sure of their plans. However, Willow was relatively thin and tall and loved to dance. Her name meaning, "graceful," designed her to become a prospective dancer.

The Myer family always enjoyed celebrating the holidays. Easter and that holy week was a fundamental way of emphasizing the core of their faith; the death and resurrection of Jesus Christ. Thanksgiving usually included a huge carry-in affair with the aunts, uncles, and cousins on Mother's side. But Christmas was the ultimate celebration for the immediate family.

The Christmas during Cedric's senior year remained most memorable. The usual plans included a lavish meal, decorating extravagantly, and making numerous candies. But this holiday was unique and demanded much thought and creativity.

Each person, parents included, was given fifty dollars to design, purchase, or make a gift for the other six family members. Dad portioned out the amounts on October 1 with the instruction to not waste time. Three months may seem long but can evaporate quickly.

Dorinda ("creative, a gift of God") knew her plans that first day. Poor Willis was still struggling on November 15. But slowly, all settled on their project and began work secretively. Each presented the following gifts on Christmas day:

Dad gave each a highly polished silver hub cap with the person's name, the meaning of that name and birth date stenciled on it.

Mom recorded herself singing a love song that best reminded her of why she loved that person.

Cedric had designed next year's calendar with monthly pictures of each family member, including his parent's anniversary.

Dorinda chose to oil-paint caricatures of each person with some comedic twist.

Rowena framed photos of different places around the world she thought that person might wish to visit someday.

Willis selected Mason quart jars to fill with candies, nuts and treats preferred by each.

Willow purchased bath towels of various colors and stitched the person's name on theirs.

It drew the Myer family closer by the thoughtfulness of the giver. The value of the gift had nothing to do with the monetary expense. It was the love shown that impressed all.

Cedric and Carma began spending more time together. They were identified as a couple by many. Dating was most often an evening at each other's home, and double dating with Bob and Monica occurred frequently. Carma and Cedric discussed some plans for the future.

"Carma are you planning to go to college after graduation?" asked Cedric.

"I may look into a community college. I'm not sure."

"I think I'll work at least a year for Dad at his shop," stated Cedric

"I don't think I'm ready to get married for a couple of years," Carma added.

"I agree. I need to build up some funds first."

Cedric suggested going on a Spring break weekend trip to Nashville to see the Grand Ole Opry. Bob and Monica were asked to travel with them as a four-some.

"Do you think our parents would let us go unchaperoned?" asked Carma.

"They might if we promise to separate girls and boys for sleeping arrangements," said Bob.

"I don't think my parents will mind. They trust me," said Monica.

All liked Country Music and the excitement built about such a venture. The parents of each person had concerns but ultimately gave consent for them to go to Nashville.

The trip was all they had hoped for and more. The sites visited and the Opry was worth the cost. For Cedric and Carma, there was an increasing bond. They managed to keep their intimacies from going all the way, but it was a test.

Upon returning home, preparations for prom and graduation stepped up. Cedric agreed to forego his class prom to attend Carma's. Bob and Monica did the same since the girls attended the same high school.

Bob and Cedric parked their cars at Central High School on prom night. They shared the expense of a limousine to pick up the girls and escort them to the prom. It was a magical night for all.

Carma's pink gown, hairstyle, and makeup made her look like a fairy-tale princess. Cedric led her with his arm into the gym decorated with streamers and sparkling lights. When the music began, the two of them held each other close and danced across the floor.

"You are so beautiful tonight, Carma."

"And you are my handsome prince."

"I love you very much."

Carma grasped Cedric, drawing him tight to her. They could not get enough of each other. Several dances did allow Bob to dance with Carma and Cedric with Monica. But Cedric's eyes were always searching for his sweetheart.

The modified cafeteria was the site of a meal after the dance. Cedric then picked up Carma with his Mercury, taking her to her house to change into more casual clothes. He put on less formal clothing, and they returned uptown to cruise with most other prom attendees.

At about 11 PM, Cedric drove up Alford's hill to a favorite parking place overlooking the town. The evening's romance led the couple to hug and kiss with increasing intensity. Finally, it had reached a boiling point.

"Cedric, I don't want to wait any longer; let's make love."

"O Carma, I've dreamt of this moment for some time."

But at that moment, the "walls" of Cedric's conscience made him consider the possible results.

"What if you get pregnant, Carma, or get VD?"

And as strong as the urge was, his mind remembered Joseph's biblical story when tempted by Potiphar's wife.

"How then can I do such a thing and sin against God?" (Genesis 39:9b)

"I'm sorry, I just can't do it."

The drive back to Carma's house was without conversation. She ran into the house crying. It was a sad ending to what had been a perfect evening. Cedric went to his bed but could not sleep.

It was three long days before Cedric called Carma. He expressed regret for the way that evening ended. Cedric apologized for his part in leading her toward such an awkward moment. He asked if they could meet the next day. Her response was a reluctant affirmative. At their meeting, Carma's demeanor was embarrassingly distant. They parted without resolving the issue between them.

Cedric graduated the following Friday with honors. His family congratulated his achievement and encouraged him to pursue his dreams. But his mind mulled over what that meant with the widening gulf between himself and Carma.

He went to work full-time at his Father's business for the summer. Having completed his accounting and business studies, he asked Dad to allow him to focus on the office. His father had more of a "shoebox" method of filing paperwork. Cedric organized a four-drawer file cabinet and categorized vendor and customer bills. Sales and billings were itemized and adequately entered into an updated bookkeeping system.

Father saw the benefits of having Cedric's assistance. He thought of more ways to prepare his son for the business's eventual ownership. Cedric's compensation increased. And two weeks after getting his diploma, he was gifted with a 1957 Robin Egg Blue Chevy Bellaire. Not only was this a surprise, but it was also Cedric's dream car.

Now nineteen years old, Cedric wondered about adulthood. Was being a mechanic and car salesman the right career for him? How long should he remain under his parent's roof? Where was the relationship with Carma heading? These were all about to be answered.

In mid-June, a letter and a small box came by courier, addressed to Cedric Myer. He was unprepared for its contents. Carma had sent the letter. It read:

Cedric,

I am writing to inform you of a decision I have made. I believed we had a very promising future together. However, as a result of some events leading up to and on prom night, that has changed.

I was ready to give myself to you, and your response was hurtful and demeaning. I felt that you not only rejected my love but for me as a person as well. I want to share my life with someone who has similar values and goals that I have. I must be honest with you. Bob and I are dating. We have both had some attraction since the Spring trip to Nashville.

Good luck with your life.

Carma

P.S. Your ring is in the box.

It was a train crash moment. A variety of emotions overcame Cedric. He informed his dad that he needed to go somewhere and was unsure he would return home that evening. Sensing his son's need for space Father wisely approved.

Cedric sped out of town toward the interstate and headed toward Indy. Thirty minutes of driving brought him to a truck stop where he parked his car. Many different response scenarios raced through his mind. Pulling out the letter, he read it twice.

The heartbreak of losing Carma brought a flood of tears. A sense of regret followed this for refusing her offer on prom night. Who would have known, he mused, and he knew the answer. Burning anger replaced these thoughts with the betrayal by his supposed best friend, Bob. Desire to take revenge rolled in his head.

Except for the loss's sorrow, the other considerations countered the character walls built into his conscience. What to do next was a big question. What would he tell his family, and what if he should meet Bob?

With tears in his eyes, he cried out to God, "Help!"

Returning home early the following day, Cedric waited for his family to wake. Mom was the first, and he told her that it was over with Carma.

She hugged him, saying, "I'm so sorry."

Dad was equally supportive and said, "Take the day off; you need to regroup."

All the siblings liked Carma and were disappointed. Cedric gave no details regarding the breakup, and they did not push for information. He had little appetite for the next four weeks, and he threw himself into his work. He became reclusive, avoiding the company of other people. Cedric repeatedly weighed his options.

At the end of July, Cedric had settled on a course of action. He returned Carma's ring without comment. At Sunday's dinner, Cedric shared with his family that he planned on moving to Colorado. A lodge near Estes Park would be his employer. None wanted him to leave but understood the difficulty and pain of being close to Bob and Carma.

On August 1, Cedric loaded his 1957 Chevy with personal possessions, and after saying goodbyes, he hit the road west. The ending of his second decade had ushered him into manhood. He only hoped the third would gracefully furnish life inside his walls.

CHAPTER 3

Furnishings

The first glimpse of the Rocky Mountains brought Cedric wonderment. A glorious vision of grandeur panned across the western horizon. Towering peaks along Big Thompson Canyon highway with its tall green pines were incredible. The rippling river along the side of the road looked refreshing and deliciously pure. Yet, it produced a sound of hidden power.

What attracted Cedric to Estes Park? The Christmas photo from Rowena was snow-capped peaks surrounding it, dwarfing the picturesque town. That scene became imprinted in Cedric's mind and inspired him to explore it someday. What better place to find a renewal of his spirit.

Exiting the top of Thompson Canyon Highway revealed Rowena's photo replica. Pulling to the side of the highway, he drank in the view for several minutes. Driving through town, he headed out route 66 to find the YMCA of the Rockies.

It was a large facility providing meeting rooms, lodging, and meals for large and small groups. Cedric checked in with the HR Director, Mr. Bradford, to complete employment papers and receive his housing assignment. Work began Monday in the maintenance department position that included many duties, from furniture setup to toilet plunging. The job had the fringe benefits of room and board.

A cabin with four separate roomettes became Cedric's housing. Included was a central living room/kitchenette and one bathroom for four guys. This arrangement was preferable over a tent, given that bears roamed the area. Most meals were served in the employee's cafeteria, while the cabin kitchen provided a place to prep snack foods.

Cedric went to a payphone to let his family know of his arrival. Mom answered the phone, and he conveyed the basics and promised to send more details in writing. With the weekend free, he composed his first letter.

August 4, 1967

Dear family,

Having died and gone to heaven, I, Cedric Myer, now bequeath the following. My former bedroom I leave to Willis. Willow can have the record player for her music. To Rowena, a big thank you for turning me on to the Rocky Mountains. To Dorinda and Rowena, I give the Mercury. Mom and Dad, I am grateful for your blessing and understanding as I seek my life's direction.

I have no idea how long I'll be here or when I might be back to visit. Till then I will write and would appreciate letters from you as well.

Love,

Cedric

P. S. I'm serious about the car. Ask Dad for the keys and take care of the old girl.

That first weekend in Colorado, Cedric began exploring the town. He picked up some information at the Visitor's Center and ate some rocky mountain oysters at the Stampede. After attending services at the YMCA chapel, Cedric entered Rocky Mountain National Park, heading for Bear Lake. A walking path circled the lake, and he was privileged to see bluegill jumping to catch insects. Chipmunks and various birds begged for food from the tourists.

Monday morning, the maintenance manager, Harvey, gathered twelve workers. He assigned four to a mowing crew, two did repair tasks, and two had painting projects to accomplish. The rest, including Cedric, headed to the convention hall to set up chairs, tables, and a stage for the incoming Mennonite Youth Fellowship.

Cedric enjoyed the physical labor and the other four workers' comradeship. He particularly appreciated Jay, who became a good friend while at the YMCA. In time others also provided some social opportunities. The absence of his family and church friends left him feeling lonely.

Jay asked Cedric, "Why don't you come with me, Curtis, and Pete Saturday night."

"Where are you going?"

"We'd like to take you for a night on the town in Boulder."

Not quite sure what all that meant, Cedric agreed to go. Pete would be the driver in his Charger. They left the YMCA around 5 PM. After driving around town for an hour, they pulled into Gilley's, a restaurant/bar on the west edge. It was a dive of a place with loud music, smoke, and many single women.

The waitress took drink orders, and Pete chided, "C'mon Ced, get you a real man's drink."

"I've never had alcohol; I'm not sure what to order."

"Get a shot of Jack Daniels; I'll buy the first round," Curtis offered.

"Sure, I'll try one." With that, Cedric crossed a line he would regret.

The guys ordered burgers, fries, and of course, more drinks. Curtis and Pete prodded Cedric to try a shot of Vodka and a Margarita chaser. The three hours at Gilley's turned into a night of partying with various female patrons for the other guys, but Cedric tried to stay to himself.

He realized that he was slowly getting dizzy and somewhat slurred in speaking. The evening began becoming blurred.

Jay later told Cedric, "You became quite vulgar and "friendly" with a girl who joined you in the booth."

It was close to 11:30 PM when they crawled into Pete's Charger for the trip back to Estes Park. The winding trip up the mountain was testing. A miscalculation could have been fatal for all.

"I don't feel so good," Cedric mumbled.

Halfway home, he vomited in the back seat. He didn't recall getting into bed but woke there still dressed in the previous night's clothes. A couple of lipstick stains on his shirt gave credence to Jay's tale. His head ached horribly.

As he thought of last evening's events, shame and a lot of guilt came over Cedric. He not only had violated his position of total abstinence, but he had seriously tarnished his witness with his friends who were non-Christians. Saying sorry wouldn't be enough. Trying to make an excuse would be lame.

When Pete woke up, he threw a bucket at Cedric and said, "You can clean up my car."

"I'll get right on it. Sorry Pete."

꧁ • ꧂

Cedric shuffled to various tasks for the balance of the year and into Spring. In November, Harvey asked him to become the events setup crew leader. As Winter approached, everyone in the department took on snow removal duties. And the Rockies had lots of snow.

Knowing that this job was not his career plan, Cedric enrolled at the University of Colorado, Boulder campus. He selected the Accounting School course leading to a CPA license. It was a combined correspondence and on-campus training. Two days per month required meeting with senior economic majors or a professor to review his progress.

Cedric devoted at least two hours per day to his studies. On weekends he often studied four hours to complete the course earlier. By Christmas, he was two months ahead of the pace.

Cedric did not wish to be a hermit. He spent time with his cabin buds playing cards and watching TV. Approximately once per week, he and Jay would head to Loveland or Boulder to shop, take in a show, and of course, find a good restaurant. They didn't waste the opportunity to observe some female "eye candy." Cedric was not interested in going beyond just looking. And he didn't order any more mixed drinks. Jay seemed to understand his struggle and respected his beliefs.

Monthly letters kept the family updated. The letters from home were always appreciated. While Dad seldom wrote, Mom sent a card weekly. Dorinda and Rowena alternately sent letters once a month. Willis managed a card about every other month due to Mom's prodding. But it was Willow who gave extra effort, sending either a letter or card weekly. Hers were always heartfelt words of encouragement to her big brother.

When Spring came, Cedric requested the chance to be placed on the mowing crew. His request was approved when one from last year's team resigned. A sixty-inch deck John Deere became his partner for the summer and fall.

Cedric turned twenty in 1968 and asked Jay to join him on a weekend trip to Fort Collins. A 4th of July rodeo was in progress and promised a new experience for both. Calf roping and bull riding were thrilling events to watch. But it was the barrel racing that intrigued Cedric most. The girls on those high-spirited steeds put on an exciting show. Of particular interest was #48. She was a slender dark-haired rider on a beautiful Palomino mare.

Preliminary rounds on Saturday advanced the four highest-scoring contestants. Sunday's competition would determine a winner. The dark-haired girl would race on Sunday.

In the first Sunday heats, #48 had the second-fastest time. She faced a runoff with the fastest-timed girl. In the final race, the Palomino edged out the roan horse by one length. The master of ceremonies announced the winner as Regina Murphy of Masonville, Colorado.

Cedric's strange feeling came as he watched #48 exit the arena with her trophy. But a more persuasive voice warned him to be careful. He said nothing to Jay of his interest. His dreams that night returned to the rodeo repeatedly.

Mom and Dad Myer drove to Colorado to visit Cedric at the end of July. It was an excellent time to show them the town and the National Park. All of them enjoyed the Lazy B western dinner show. Their time went quickly, and they needed to return to Indiana.

It was great to see his parents. Dad, however, wanted to question Cedric about coming home for the sake of the business. Cedric stated that it wasn't likely, particularly since starting at the University of Colorado. Mom expressed concern at his loss of weight, wanting assurances that he was OK. Though disappointed, they understood Cedric was where he belonged.

By semester's end in December, Cedric had passed year two of the accounting program. With grades near the top of the scale and accelerated progress, his professor suggested Cedric seek a position at an accounting firm. This move would give him a practical application and provide experience on his resume.

With referral and transcripts in hand, he conducted interviews in Loveland and one in Fort Collins. Cedric agreed to an employment arrangement with Brookstone and Kelly Accounting of Fort Collins. Cedric submitted his resignation from the YMCA effective December 31 and moved to a one-bedroom apartment in Fort Collins.

෨ • ಇ

Wishing to establish a community presence and reconnect with a vibrant church, Cedric visited several. He felt most at home and in theological agreement with the Evangelical Free Church (EFC) on West Cedar Street. It was a church of nearly 150 members.

On his second Sunday at Fort Collins EFC, he was pleasantly surprised to see Regina Murphy listed as a soloist. The name resonated a memory in his mind, but he wasn't sure why. That was until she came onto the platform to sing. There behind the microphone was the Palomino girl. In a gold satin dress with flowing black hair, she sang, "It Is Well with My Soul," as the choir provided backup. She performed flawlessly, and her appearance was equally perfect.

The discovery thrilled Cedric. Their meeting was not accidental, piquing his interest to know her better. Upon leaving the church, she was standing near the door as an exit greeter.

"Hi, I'm Regina. What is your name?"

"My name is Cedric."

"Are you a first-time visitor with us today?"

"This is my second Sunday here."

"I hope to see you back. Here is a packet about Fort Collins Church."

"I enjoyed the service, and I will be back."

While eating lunch at Applebees, he perused the packet. He saw the name, Carl Murphy, Chairman of the Elder Board, and wondered if he was Regina's Father or another relative. A program listing indicated a college-age singles group met. Maybe their paths might cross again, soon he hoped.

Work at Brookstone and Kelly began the following day. Frank Brookstone met him at the entrance and gave a thorough tour, with introductions to each staff member. He showed Cedric the office he would be using.

"I'll let you get settled, and then I will bring you a project to work on," stated Frank.

"Thank you. I'm anxious to get started."

Being the first of the year meant it was time to assist clients with income tax preparations. Tax accounting was Cedric's specialty. He expected some overtime as April 15 approached. Cedric scheduled a forty-five-hour workweek to give time for continuing education. He managed to work more than that and still maintained his graduation goals.

Cedric processed many simple individual tax returns to start. He received single proprietor clients after several weeks. Then tackled his first partnership file on April 1. A senior CPA in the firm checked his work with each new step.

On April 16, the office returned to regular hours. The agency closed in the afternoon for all staff members to gather at a prestigious restaurant. Following the meal, Mr. Brookstone thanked everyone for their hard work. He then distributed a generous bonus to everyone.

Frank stated, "We are thrilled to have Cedric on staff. He has proven to be a proficient accountant. We look forward to his continuing partnership with the firm."

Cedric was overwhelmed by the compliments and monetary rewards. Dramatic changes had taken place in the last two years. He thankfully acknowledged the heavenly Father's providence and for hearing his cry for help. He honored his Lord by worship with words and a tithe of his earnings. As his name implies, he looked for ways to be generous to various people.

Fort Collins Church became more than just a Sunday gathering place. Its ministries met people's needs locally and around the world. Every member would commit themselves to serve in some ministry area. This commitment appealed to Cedric as he looked for a service option.

His first two months as an attendee provided numerous chances to meet and observe Regina. Each week increased his desire to spend private time with her, but he feared going too fast. A singles gathering sped up the process.

The bulletin announced a Friday night pizza party for the singles group. Cedric and Regina were both there. The 6:00 meal began with guys on one side of the fellowship hall and girls on the other. He glanced across the room just as she looked his way. He smiled and turned back to the boys.

At 6:45, the Youth Pastor called all to gather at the center table. Each of the twenty-four people wrote their names on a paper with numbers 1 to 24. People with odd numbers placed their names in one bowl and even numbers in another bowl. On cue, the even-numbered people picked a person's name from the odd-numbered bowl. Luckily, Regina was on the even side and Cedric on the odd-numbered side.

The intent was to ask the person selected questions to become better acquainted and share them with the group. In the first round, Emily selected Cedric's name. She was timid, and her questions were very general.

Cedric picked Regina's name in the second round. He sat across from her and carefully asked important but non-invasive questions. He found out she was an only child of a ranching family, a nineteen-year-old student at Fort Collins Community College. She liked horses and one day wanted to see the Queen of England.

Then all questioners shared the information they had gleaned. Emily struggled to recall all she had learned about Cedric. When Cedric spoke, he shared Regina's answers plus added side notes. Winning the championship trophy for barrel racing at the rodeo the previous year was one. The add-on to "wanted to see the Queen" was because her name meant "queen."

Cedric's informational add-ons struck Regina with wonderment. She realized that his interest in her went beyond the casual. Following a closing devotional, she worked her way to him before he could leave.

"You know me better than I realized," she said with a smile.

"Perhaps I find you to be quite interesting."

"I'd like to get more information on you."

"Would you let me take you to dinner Sunday?"

"I'll be ready after church."

"It's a date," Cedric replied.

With that, he smiled and left the hall. Before sleeping that night, he rehearsed all he knew about Regina and searched his motive for the attraction. There was the lure of her beauty. She displayed an aura of sincere humility and friendliness. And she showed a confident strength in her womanhood. Cedric wanted to have a deeper understanding of her.

The worship service that following Sunday was a blur. His mind struggled to think of anything but that angelic face in the choir. The final "Amen" couldn't come soon enough. When it did, he hurried to wait for her at the door. They agreed to leave her car in the church lot, and Cedric drove to the restaurant.

"Is the Blue Mountain Inn OK for lunch?" he asked.

"Oh, I love that place. My cousin is a waitress there."

"How is the food? I've only been there for breakfast once."

"They have the best seafood, and my dad likes their steaks."

"Sounds like they have a great menu."

In ten minutes, they pulled in, parked, and he opened her door. It was a busy place, and there was a five-minute wait. As they were being seated, he noticed several familiar faces. A few tables had Fort Collins Church people at them. In a booth sat Kate, the receptionist from Brookstone. Suddenly he felt all eyes were on them. So much for privacy.

Regina ordered the shrimp scampi dinner with a coke. Cedric preferred steak but didn't want to look famished. He chose the codfish combo. It was simple and hopefully safe to avoid slurping and less messy.

"Tell me about your family," Regina requested.

"My mom, dad, a brother, and three sisters live in northern Indiana."

"What kind of work do your folks do?" she asked.

"Dad owns a service station and car dealership. Mom is a nurse at the local hospital," Cedric replied.

"And your siblings, are they older or younger than you."

"I'm the oldest, then sisters, Dorinda and Rowena follow me. After them, the Twins, Willis and Willow, came along.

"So why did you leave Indiana and come to Colorado? Regina questioned.

He gave her the condensed version of his biography without some challenging issues. She wanted to hear more but felt it might be too prying.

"Tell me about your family," Cedric inquired.

"As you know, I'm an only child. My dad is Carl, and my mom's name is Janice. We live just outside Masonville on a 2,500-acre ranch in the foothills of the Rockies."

"Are you working or in college?"

"I'm in the community college intending to become a dental hygienist," said Regina.

Her interest in horses was life-long. She was born and raised around them, getting her first pony at age four, a large horse at eleven, and trained for barrel racing at age fourteen.

"What did you mean at the singles party that you knew about my winning the championship at the July 4th rodeo?" asked Regina.

"My friend Jay and I were at the rodeo both Saturday and Sunday. We saw you win. Something about you drew my attention, and your name stuck in my mind."

"And you remembered me six months later?"

"You were hard to forget," Cedric replied seductively.

Regina blushed as she gave her proverbial smile. Cedric wondered if he was too forward, but he decided to take a chance.

"I did a little research to find out your name means "queen." Do you have any royal blood in your line?"

"Not that I'm aware. I don't think I'm in line for the crown."

"Well, you still deserve to see her Royal Highness."

The date was exhilarating for Cedric. It was easy to converse with Regina. He regretted seeing their time end.

When dropping her off at her car, he asked, "Will I see you next Sunday?"

"I will look forward to it."

When Regina arrived home, her parents probed for a report.

She replied with a grin, "The food was fabulous."

"Only the food?" asked her mother.

"Well, the company was OK too."

"So, will you be seeing him again?" questioned her father.

"He said he would be at church next week, so I guess I will."

Both Regina and Cedric spent the night contemplating the importance of their outing and whether there was a future together or would it remain at a friendship level. Neither was ready to throw caution to the wind. A night's sleep might help to clarify.

At work the following day, Kate tried to pry for more information.

"Who was that cute gal you were with at Blue Mountain?" she asked.

"Oh, you didn't recognize my sister?" he said as he headed to his office.

"Sister, my eye," she laughed. "You don't open the car door for a sister."

Kate could hear Cedric chuckling as he entered his office.

The workload demanded that Cedric give full attention to avoid making erroneous entries. He couldn't help wondering what the appropriate next step should be. A telephone call might be too aggressive, a bouquet a little presumptuous, but a single rose and a card could convey his heart. He had them delivered to Regina's door on Wednesday.

The card said, "Simply Cedric."

On Sunday morning, Cedric arrived early, seating himself in a middle row to the far right. He spent time praying, meditating, and waiting for Regina. With a tap on his shoulder, he heard Regina ask,

"Is that seat reserved?"

"Yes, I think your name was on that seat."

Regina slid into the pew, and Cedric sat next to her. The worship service was a powerful experience. Both sang joyfully and in harmony. The preacher's sermon was titled "The Essentials of Love." After the service, they found a corner in the back to talk.

"Thank you for the rose and card," Regina whispered.

"I wanted you to know I enjoyed being with you."

"In two weeks from today, would you come home with me for dinner?"

"I'd consider it an honor and privilege."

Cedric felt like he was floating on a cloud. He threw himself into his work and tried to pick up progress on his studies. Physically he was a little weary, but emotionally he was at peace.

&) • CR

To find his way to the Murphy home Regina came to church with her parents and rode with Cedric to guide him. The ranch entrance sign said, "Welcome to Murphy's Eden Ranch," with the "ME" brandmark below. The house was a half-mile off the highway. It stood in front of a large barn, several sheds, and a bunkhouse. The peaks of the Rockies were a backdrop to this scene.

Upon entering the house, Cedric was welcomed warmly by Mrs. Murphy. Regina's dad came out of the den, reached out his hand, and shook Cedric's with a good grip.

"We are glad to finally meet you Cedric," said Carl.

"It's my pleasure to meet you as well. Thank you for the invitation."

"The credit goes to Regina. Any friend of hers is welcome here."

Janice called out, "Dinner is ready. Please come take a seat."

The aroma of a home-cooked meal filled the room; it reminded him of home. The table setting included large porcelain plates, crystal goblets, various Western motif napkins, silverware, spice, and condiment containers. Mr. and Mrs. Murphy sat on one side of the rectangular table, putting Regina and Cedric on the other.

Mr. Murphy offered the prayer of thanks. A garden salad and warm homemade bread was the first course. Carl and Janice asked questions to acquaint the Murphys with the man pursuing their daughter. It was less an inquisition and more a sincere attempt to show interest in Cedric as a person. After collecting the salad dishes, Mrs. Murphy brought baked potatoes, baked beans, and a platter with six large rib-eye steaks. Dessert would come as an afternoon treat.

Cedric feeling so at home, began relaxing. He offered to help clean up the table, but Janice chased the guys to the den. More questions were informative to both men.

"When will you finish your schoolwork at the university?" asked Carl

"I plan to have my pre-CPA completed in December."

"You and Regina will both graduate this year."

Cedric wondered if Carl's statement carried more profound implications. Was a long-term friendship with Regina what her father anticipated? The next topic of conversation could hint at Cedric's possible desire to develop a relationship with Regina.

"I understand you are chairman of the Board of Elders at the Fort Collins Church," said Cedric.

"Yes, I am one of six, including Pastor Houser."

"What is the process to become a church member?"

"A referral to the Elders for approval follows a four-week class. The next class starts in May. Would you like an application?"

"Yes. I believe Fort Collins Church has what I'm looking for," he said just as Regina and her mother entered the room.

Mr. Murphy suggested that the four take a ride around the ranch in the Land Rover. Cedric brought some jeans, a casual shirt, and boots to wear. He had purchased a pair the previous Friday. All of them exchanged their Sunday clothes for appropriate ranch duds. Regina looked like an authentic cowgirl.

In corrals were cows and newly branded calves. They were waiting for release in May to higher pastures. As they drove, Regina pointed to various sites she liked to ride.

The Rover took them across a creek, then climbed up into the foothills. In the distance, there were some elk. They saw the ranch house below and the city of Masonville a few miles beyond. The view was breathtaking.

On the way back about a mile from the house, they came upon a moderately sized cabin. It had electrical service lines that came from the barn below.

"Who lives there?" asked Cedric.

"That's Paradise Retreat. It's a get-away for family members and sometimes a guest house," answered Regina.

When they returned to the house, Regina asked if Cedric cared to meet her Palomino. She showed him the bunkhouse where Red Parsons, the ranch foreman, stayed along with Rex and Duely, the ranch hands. When they entered the barn, a loud whinny came from Patsy greeting Regina. She was a beautiful mare so suitable with Regina on her back.

On their way back to the house for dessert, Cedric took a deep breath and asked, "Regina, would you consider becoming my steady girlfriend?"

"I was hoping you would ask. I want to spend more time with you."

Reaching out, he took her hand. Squeezing it gently, they looked into each other's eyes. To commemorate their steady relationship, Cedric purchased two silver heart halves on necklaces. He gave Regina half with his name and kept the other with hers. He inscribed the date when this friendship started.

Cedric knew the time had come to contact his family. A prearranged telephone call took place at 8:00 PM (EST). With a conference call device, the whole family could hear Cedric's voice.

Since he moved to Fort Collins, Cedric and his family usually called every Sunday evening. He told them about his work and social activities. They, in turn, gave information about events back in Indiana.

Following the dinner at the Murphy home, he told them about his new friend, Regina. Immediately there came a chorus of congratulations and questions.

Mom said, "I could tell you sounded happier and upbeat."

"When can we meet her?" Rowena wanted to know.

Cedric baited them teasingly, "That depends when you can come and visit me."

Mom added, "I hope we can meet Regina soon. Well, it's almost our bedtime here; we'll talk on your birthday next week."

In the cards, for Cedric's twenty-first birthday, a note from Dorinda stated that Rowena was arranging airline tickets for some time in July.

Cedric suggested, "Consider the week of July 4 to see Regina in the rodeo."

Regina and Cedric dated quite regularly. He invited her to his apartment for a simple meal of chicken tenders, tater tots, and peas on his birthday. Lemon meringue pie would be the dessert. At the end of dinner, he revealed that it was his birthday. Regina was embarrassed because she did not know it was his birthday and had failed to get him a gift.

"That's OK. I wanted to surprise you."

"Well, I won't forget next year," Regina promised.

Through the summer and fall, they usually ate out weekly. Select dates included a Steve and Annie Chapman concert in Denver, trips to Pikes Peak and Rocky Mountain National Park. On several occasions, Cedric rode horseback at the ranch. He had a lot to learn about horses.

On July 1, Cedric traveled to Denver International Airport to pick up Dorinda and Rowena. He gave them a big bear hug.

Willow slipped up behind him and said, "Hi, Cedric."

Whirling around, Cedric exclaimed, "Willow! You came too!"

He hugged her joyfully. They went to baggage claim, picked up their luggage, then left the airport.

Cedric reserved a motel in Fort Collins for his sisters near his apartment. Regina joined them for a Pizza supper, and the ladies hit it off from the start.

The rodeo was exciting for Cedric and his sisters. The girls were amazed at Regina's skill in barrel racing. She repeated the previous year's outcome by being the champion.

Cedric showed his sisters Estes Park and the National Park. On the sixth day of their visit, it was time for their return home.

Rowena commented, "I like Regina. When's the wedding?"

"Tomorrow," Cedric replied as he laughed

"You will keep us informed, won't you?" Willow asked seriously.

"I might drop a card to you."

"It better be more than a card. I want an invitation of my own," demanded Dorinda.

Following the girl's visit, Cedric and Regina's lives returned to their everyday routines. Regina's classes and internship were proceeding well. December 15 was her graduation date. Cedric's accounting class neared completion at about the same time. Mr. Brookstone assigned him seven key clients to oversee their bookkeeping and prepare state and federal reports.

With November 10 coming, Cedric made plans for Regina's twentieth birthday. He secured reservations at The Lamplighter, an upscale restaurant in Loveland. He invited Carl and Janice to join them. Now came the dilemma of choosing her gift.

Cedric set up an appointment in October with Mr. Murphy at the ranch while Regina was in school. With humble confidence, he asked Carl if he could bless and grant Regina's marriage to himself.

"I couldn't think of anyone else. I'd like you to be my daughter's husband. That is, if she will want you," Carl replied with a smile.

"Well, that is the next hurdle."

Cedric explained his plans to ask Regina to marry him at the birthday party. They discussed a surprise twist with the offering of the diamond. Cedric needed to make a purchase.

On November 10, Mr. Murphy volunteered to escort them all in his Olds 88 to the restaurant. The reservation included a somewhat secluded section of The Lamplighter. The delicious meal came with a special cake. After dinner, Mr. Murphy pulled a small box from his suit coat, handing it to Regina. In it, she found keys to a 1969 Mustang. It was her combination birthday and graduation gift.

"Oh, Mom and Dad, this is so generous of you. Thank you."

"You are our special girl and worth it," replied Janice.

Cedric spoke hesitatingly, "Wow, Mr. Murphy, you set the bar high. But I did get you something smaller, Regina."

With that, he stood up as if to go after the gift. Instead, he walked to Regina's chair, went to his knee, and asked her to marry him. He handed her a box with the diamond ring. Regina gasped then jumped up to hug Cedric.

Before she could say "yes," as prearranged, Mr. Murphy stood up and sternly asked, "What? Who said you could take my daughter?"

"You did, sir," Cedric said submissively.

"Oh, guess I did," Carl said with a laugh.

Both Cedric and Carl smiled at the joke. Regina and her mother didn't know whether to laugh or smack their men.

Instead, Regina turned again to Cedric, saying, "Yes, Yes, forever YES!"

Regina had given Cedric several kisses since they began dating steadily. But this kiss was firm and passionate. Extreme happiness and excitement about the future filled everyone.

Cedric called Indiana the following day. He wanted to scream out the news but decided to milk the moment with jest. He began speaking, sounding somewhat deflated. A few in his family thought this might be a repeat of a few years earlier.

"Hi everyone." sounding sad, "I took a chance and popped the question to Regina, and she said," and delayed momentarily, "YES!"

From Indiana, there were screams of "yeah, yeah."

"When is the wedding going to take place?" Willow wanted to know.

"We have to talk and decide on a date. Are you free next week?"

His family was delighted. They were happy to hear Cedric's spirit in such a revived mood. Dad and Willis were a little more reserved but said they would be there.

Saturday, June 20, 1970, became the selected wedding date. The ranch would be the setting, and Rev. Houser agreed to officiate. Cedric and Regina mailed the invitations to family and friends.

Six months seemed like an eternity to wait. But time was needed for the many preparations and events to take place. Regina's graduation and the start of her work at

Fort Collins Dental Services was one. Pre-marital counseling was another. The selection of wedding party attendants and their outfits required additional work.

With Regina's graduation being December 15, Cedric asked her if the week between Christmas and New Year would work for them to fly to Indiana. The trip would be Cedric's first time back since coming to Colorado. His immediate and extended family would have the opportunity to meet his fiance.

The trip was a great success. Regina asked Dorinda and Rowena to be matrons of honor with Willow to facilitate guest sign-in and gift recording. Mom Myer consented to sing a solo, and Willis would stand up with his brother. Dad agreed to pick up the tab for the rehearsal supper.

In early December, Cedric and Regina discussed personal issues regarding where to live, vocational plans, and the number of children desired. Ultimately they addressed the subject of sexual intimacy.

Regina inquired, "Do you see this white ring I wear on my left pinky?"

"Yes, I wondered what it symbolized."

"At a banquet when I was fifteen, Dad and I listened to a speaker about sex and the importance of waiting till marriage. I came to understand why God designed sex as a good thing at the right time. I vowed to do it in God's way. So I was given this "ring of purity" to remind me of that promise and help me have the strength to say "no" till then."

"Have you ever been tempted to give in?"

"I'm human. My resolve has gone through a test."

Cedric related the story of him and Carma and how close they came to give in. It was this test that led him to Colorado. Satan's attempt to violate God's child became a blessing by bringing Regina into his life. Tears of joy filled both their eyes. They kissed each other, but just a peck for safety's sake.

The pace became furious from January through May 1970. Few leisure hours remained after wedding planning, Cedric's tax preparation, and Regina's work at the dental clinic. But the couple kept priorities straight, providing time for each other.

The day had finally arrived. Many hands cleaned the ranch thoroughly. Erection of a tent large enough to accommodate 250 guests took place in a meadow near the house. Families came from various parts of the country. And the weather was perfect with temps in the high sixties at the 11 AM start.

A western dress motif was the suggested attire for all attendees and the wedding party. In addition to cowboy boots, male attendants had dressed in black suits, ruffled shirts, ribbon ties, and broad-rimmed hats. Lady attendants wore knee-length gingham dresses. A surrey brought the bride from the back of the house, driven by her father.

She wore a white knee-length dress, white boots, a lace-trimmed hat, and a cameo around her neck.

Daddy walked his daughter down the aisle to "Always" by Patsy Cline and the Jordanaires. The ceremony lasted forty-five minutes. Rev. Houser combined humorous anecdotes with biblical challenges. The couple using a lariat, tied a knot to a saddle horn to symbolize their union. He concluded the ceremony by having the couple face the attendees.

"I now present to you, Mr. and Mrs. Cedric and Regina Myer."

Everyone burst into exuberant cheers and clapped. As they exited the tent, Regina's Palomino and Cedric's black stallion were waiting. The couple mounted and circled once around the meadow.

The tent emptied, and men set up tables for the meal. Conestoga Caterers provided a chuck wagon dinner complete with tin trays. Guests enjoyed steak, a potato, beans, dinner roll, and a peach half. They served wedding cake following the dance. A western music group played during the meal and for the dance.

Gifts were taken into the house to be opened and recorded with the two immediate families the following afternoon. The wedding couple walked around trying to greet and thank each guest. Most had departed by 4 PM.

At 5 PM, the first part of the honeymoon began. Foreman Red Parson picked up the couple at the ranch in the surrey, and they were taken up the lane to Paradise Retreat. Their overnight bags were delivered to the cabin early that morning. Stocking the kitchen with drinks, snacks, and breakfast foods was Mom Murphy's work. The bedroom and bath contained scented candles. Everything was ready for a romantic night.

Cedric helped his bride out of the carriage, up the porch, and opened the front door. He scooped Regina in his arms and carried her across the threshold, closing and locking the door. With matches in hand, they lit all the candles.

They turned toward one another, their hearts pounding with excited expectation. Simultaneously they watched the other disrobing. The purity ring was the last item that Regina removed. She stepped up to Cedric and placed the ring in his hand.

"I give you this ring to symbolize the gift of my body to you."

The consummation of their marriage permitted the exploration of virgin territory without shame or guilt. Though awkward from inexperience, it fulfilled the hunger for love's desire and provided them the bliss of physical pleasure.

> *"A wife of noble character who can find? She is worth far more than rubies. Her husband has full confidence in her and lacks nothing in value."* Proverbs 31:10-11

Unaccustomed to sleeping with another person, Regina and Cedric woke periodically through the night. At one point, the full moon showed through the window, waking them. Clasping each other, they embraced again.

Cedric asked if Regina was interested in a whirlpool bath with him in the morning.

"I would love it."

"I'll fill it up for us."

"And I'll bring some fruit and cheese for us to eat while we relax," Regina said.

They spent the rest of the morning talking about the wedding, snacking on food, and rekindling their fire. After dressing for the day, they walked the mile to the house arriving at 1 PM.

"How did the newlyweds sleep?" asked Janice

Regina, smiling sheepishly, quipped, "Together."

"Well, I presumed you would. Are you hungry?"

"I'll have some coffee," Cedric said.

"I can wait till later," answered Regina.

The rest of the Myer family returned at 2:30. Regina and Cedric opened their gifts as Willow kept a record. They received many household goods, small appliances, linens, decorative items, and monetary donations. Each item was sincerely appreciated, with thank you cards mailed after the honeymoon.

Following a 5:00 PM supper, the Indiana Myer family said their "goodbyes," returning to their motel and heading home the following day. Cedric and Regina spent a second night at Paradise Retreat, then loaded their Chevy for a 2:00 PM flight out of Denver. The second part of their honeymoon destination was still a secret to Regina.

After a plane change in New York, Regina realized they were on an international flight to London. Cedric revealed that they had an audience with Her Majesty the Queen.

"You said you wanted to see her someday," Cedric noted.

"It was just a fantasy. I never thought it would come true."

"My queen deserves to have her dream become a reality."

He explained that the trip was made possible by the Brookstone Accounting firm. Combined with that year's bonus and staff contributions, they gave an all-expense-paid five-day stay in England and Scotland. The queen only made a public balcony wave from Buckingham Palace.

The guided tours allowed them to see many of the famous sites of Great Brittan. Their favorite venture was an evening dinner cruise with lights illuminating London's buildings. All too soon, it was time to return to work.

A month before the wedding, Cedric and Regina had signed a purchase agreement for a three-bedroom house. Located between Fort Collins and Masonville on a ten-acre plot, its small barn would enable the Palomino's boarding. It was ideal for their needs.

The house was painted and cleaned. Then furniture, appliances, and window treatments were installed before Carl and Janice delivered the wedding gifts. The returning couple found it ready to move in.

The rest of the summer was a time of establishing routines and making adjustments to the married lifestyle. They were unprepared for a surprise in September. Regina was pregnant. It might have been unplanned, but the couple was joyful at the prospect of parenting.

℘ • ℆

With joy also comes sorrow in life. Disappointing news came in the form of a miscarriage the first week of October. The loss was particularly hard for Regina's mother, who had experienced a miscarriage before Regina and two after her. The doctors determined that her uterine wall could not support childbearing, and she had a hysterectomy. Janice feared that her daughter might have inherited similar conditions.

Cedric's involvement at the church increased. In June of 1969, he became a member. Pastor Houser suggested he serve on the Mission Commission. Cedric also took a teaching rotation for the high school class. By 1972 he occasionally led a devotional for a nursing home ministry.

Regina and Cedric's first Christmas as a married couple was delightful. Regina hosted Christmas dinner with her parents present. She was a skilled cook and baker. However, that evening Regina became ill and suspected something eaten was the culprit. She felt better the following day.

On January 20, 1971, she again felt ill. A doctor's visit determined that the problem was baby-related. This time she and Cedric kept it a secret from her mother until March. New excitement and cautious hope filled the Murphy and Myer homes, including Indiana.

On September 23, 1971, Ruth Ellen Myer was born. Her dark hair and sparkling eyes were similar to Regina's. Her cries were music to Cedric's ears, except at 2 AM. Ruth's sweet demeanor brought delight to everyone who held and cared for her.

With Grandma Murphy's assistance, Regina returned part-time to work in November. Cedric managed to supply childcare several days a month. The family bonded as they raised Ruth in an atmosphere of loving discipline.

Cedric prepared for the CPA exam with the State of Colorado. In May of 1972, he traveled to Denver for the test. He passed the exam and received his license with helpful tutoring from Frank Brookstone and practical work years.

A more significant celebration came with a son, Timothy Allen, born on December 7, 1972. Thankfully he resembled Cedric's nose and brown eyes. He would acquire his Grandpa Murphy's height starting twenty-three inches at birth.

Regina resigned from the dental service with the birth of Timothy. She wished to devote her time to nurturing her family and have greater involvement at the church. Regina accepted the worship and music director position. She helped lead congregational singing and scheduled special music groups to give concerts. She also directed the choir.

Her most notable accomplishment came with establishing the annual Living Christmas Tree musical. This eight-day presentation drew people from surrounding communities. Most notably was that new believers committed their lives to Jesus each year.

"Christmas is my favorite time of the year," Regina noted.

"You did a fantastic job of planning and conducting the Tree musical," complimented Cedric.

"It took everyone involved to make it successful."

From 1973 through most of 1976, the Myer family was in a groove of the familiar and safe. The children were growing up and healthy. Parents were busy yet happy in their roles at home, work, and community. Life was comfortably satisfying.

Then came July 31, 1976. This day shook many in the Rocky Mountain communities. Around ten inches of rain had fallen in minutes. The storm brought torrents of rain into the town of Estes Park. The streams funneled through the city and down the Big Thompson River. This beautiful, picturesque river became a monstrous water wall through the canyon to Loveland below. In its wake, roads, houses, trees, and vehicles trapped in the canyon washed downstream. Around 150 people died by the time it was over.

Following the devastation shock, the living began looking for the survivors and the dead. Construction and utility companies rushed to tediously clean up and restore, taking months and years to accomplish this feat. The scars would last a long time.

Volunteers came to help in the recovery and healing process. The Fort Collins Church board granted the Mission Commission authority to organize and oversee outreach to the Loveland Basin. Members and attendees gave donations of clothes, household items, money, and donated labor hours.

Cedric, a Mission Commission member, was given the purse strings to make the most of the $100,000.00 contribution collected that first year, prioritizing aid for individual families needing help to recover and rebuild. The scope of the suffering and God's people's generosity was humbling for Cedric.

"If anyone has material possessions and sees his brother in need but has no pity on him, how can the love of God be in him." I John 3:17

Cedric proposed an action step to the church Elder Board in contacts made with several Loveland families. His request was to consider establishing a satellite church in this devastated area. When presented to the congregation, a substantial majority affirmed the proposal.

The District Superintendent gave Fort Collins the following directions for starting a church:

1. Establish a weekly Bible study group in the area;

2. Refer a church planting pastor after at least twenty-five adults regularly attended;

3. Provide for Sunday worship meetings;

4. Ask three families from Fort Collins Church to voluntarily participate for two years.

Fort Collins scheduled a revival series for January of 1977. A well-known EFC speaker, Dr. Jack Hammer, came to Fort Collins. Throughout the four-day service, Cedric felt divine prodding through Dr. Hammer's biblical and personal challenges. On the final night, the sermon title was "Stepping Out of Your Comfort Zone." The nudging of the Holy Spirit was powerful. The altar call was for those believers whom God wanted to use for his service. Cedric stood and submitted himself to God's call.

Cedric felt sure he knew what the call meant. He and Regina talked for hours and committed themselves to prayer. They were open to God's direction without reservations.

The previous three decades provided multiple "furnishings" inside the walls of Cedric's soul. God had blessed him with meaningful relationship opportunities, accomplishments in career and ministry endeavors, and wisdom to choose good over evil.

But the enemy of the soul also seeks to rob the joy of these blessings by using them in ways that counter God's intent and design. Consequently, Cedric committed sins that left him feeling defeated and remorseful. He reminded himself of shooting his sister's hand, leading Carma toward sexual mistakes, and blowing his testimony by getting drunk in front of his friends. And despite seeking God's forgiveness, his failures latched onto his soul, increasing his doubts and guilt.

CHAPTER 4

Hat Closet

Some houses are known to have some unusual rooms. Secret rooms allow one to hide items from view. Other rooms have only single-use purposes, like the furnace room. But none is like the hat closet, frequented in one's life house to indicate the roles played at any given time.

Cedric and Regina wore their parental hats with pride and trepidation. Fatherhood was a role that Cedric took seriously. His love for Ruth and Timothy went beyond emotional feelings. His tone of words, tender hands, and tireless sacrifices for their welfare was evident. Building good character in them required him to guide and guard through life's hazardous walk.

Cedric provided his children the necessities of food, clothes, and housing. Meals were eaten together as a family, enabling sharing daily events and personal interests. Regina worked hard to prepare foods that met physical requirements and individual tastes. She also dressed them appropriately depending on the occasion and weather.

Formal education outside the home began when Ruth, at age 5, was taken to Kindergarten.

"What did you do today in school?" Cedric asked.

"We counted to twenty, and we played musical chairs, and we ate.'"

"Did you make any new friends?"

"No, we were all a bunch of old friends."

Ruth, whose name means "companion and friend," was quick to get along with all around her. For her, the school would always be a great place to be. She excelled with high-grade marks.

Timothy, however, was a pea of a different pod. Academic success did not come easily. It wasn't stubbornness or a dislike of his teachers, but some internal interference kept him from learning. Cedric and Regina spent many evenings trying to assist him with his homework. The optometrist discovered in third grade that his one problem was optical. A pair of glasses changed his perspective of the school. It didn't mean that he began getting all "A's."

Timothy, like his mother, had an affinity for the equestrian world. Regina purchased him a pony at age five. He enjoyed spending hours with Grandpa Carl range-riding and, in time, herding cattle. Calf-roping became his forte at age twelve. In 1987 he became the Junior Champion at the Fort Collins rodeo on his horse, Bandit They were great partners in outmaneuvering those elusive calves. Timothy and his mom developed a strong bond because of shared interests.

Ruth, on the other hand, preferred indoor activities. It involved playing dress-up or house in which daddy often participated with tea parties and pretended to be husband in younger years. Her friendly spirit and popularity with so many schoolmates led to her being crowned homecoming queen in her senior year. Cedric proudly claimed her as "daddy's girl."

The children's spiritual formation was of primary interest to Regina and Cedric. They were in regular attendance in Sunday School and church events. The church's teachings, coupled with open discussions at home, instilled what it meant to be a godly person. Ruth asked Jesus into her life at a Bible School program in 1981, while Timothy made his faith profession in 1987 at the Sunday morning rodeo chapel. Baptism followed for both after some instructional classes.

In 1977 Cedric helped establish a Bible study group in Matt and Cindy Davidson's home in Loveland. Seven other adults joined this start-up attempt for a possible new church. They set Sunday evening for the meeting time to maximize the potential of inviting others, allowing Fort Collins' leadership to participate without taking away from other ministry duties.

Pastor Ethan Houser asked Cedric to his office to discuss the Loveland area ministry plans.

"Well, Cedric, you have been quite busy leading the Loveland recovery."

"We have helped numerous families, thanks to Fort Collins' donations."

"I understand we are ready to establish a Bible study there."

"Yes, the Davidsons have volunteered to use their home."

"Who will be leading the group study?" inquired Pastor Ethan.

"I was hoping you might have some suggestions."

"Cedric, I've been praying and thinking. I believe you are the man."

"But I've not had any formal training. How would I begin?"

"You've taught Sunday School classes and lead devotionals at the retirement home. The feedback I've received has been very positive of your giftedness."

"What would you suggest as curriculum?"

"Well, I highly recommend the Bible. There are many guidebooks like Navpress and others."

"Talk about stepping from my comfort zone. This act may be a leap," exclaimed Cedric.

"I will always be available to encourage and guide you."

With that, Cedric put on a church planting/teacher's hat. He purchased books, and the first Sunday group met on October 2, 1977. The ten people filled the Davidson living room. From that beginning, the number grew to twenty by the end of the year.

Fort Collins Church designated the Living Christmas Tree offerings that year to the Loveland ministry. God was blessing the people and work, and 1978 would become a pivotal year for the Myer family and the Loveland Church. The following decade for Cedric would take on a pastoral focus. The significance of God's call to serve was becoming more apparent.

But with the additional work with its time demands, there were also some new stress levels on family life.

"You know that your church work has become quite consuming on Sundays," noted Regina.

"I know," said Cedric. "But I feel obligated to put my best into this new effort."

"Perhaps you can set aside Saturday entirely for the family as an alternative."

"Most weeks, it could be an option, but there will come some exceptions."

"The kids and I need you to try making it a priority as much as possible," said Regina.

Cedric tried harder to balance the demands of family and work. The increased growth of this infant church led to the leasing of a rental facility in April. The Fort Collins Church helped supply chairs, a podium, and other needed furniture to aid the needs of the Loveland Church. While the Bible study format continued into June, Sunday AM, July 2 became the goal for a traditional worship service to begin.

Several steps occurred to aid in the church's expansion. First, the name "New Life Loveland Fellowship" was adopted. Until it was officially an independent entity, the assets remained legally as a DBA (doing business as) of Fort Collins Evangelical Free Church. Second, the elders would begin the search for a church-planting pastor with the District Superintendent's help. And third was developing a marketing plan to appeal to non-churched people to check out Loveland Fellowship.

Elder Carl Murphy stated, "Who would have known that Fort Collins would have been able to start a sister church."

"Yes, and to see it as an outgrowth of such a tragic event as the flood," said Pastor Ethan.

"I'm excited about what God has in mind for Loveland Church's future," Cedric added.

The excitement was growing with each step toward the opening. The 5:00 Sunday PM time slot would be maintained for the Bible study, pending the incoming pastor's input. They interviewed two pastors for the position of Church Planting Pastor. The criteria required the person to be bi-vocational at one-half the standard salary rate until the budget grew. They chose Steven Thorp to lead New Life Loveland Fellowship beginning June 1.

Rev. Thorp was a forty-two-year-old man with a pharmaceutical degree. Melanie, a registered nurse, was his wife. They moved from California to Loveland in May.

Being childless gave them the freedom to find appropriate employment in the Loveland or Boulder area while still giving significant time for church work. Rev. Thorp had successfully helped start two churches before Loveland.

Pastor Houser convened a meeting including Rev. Thorp and Cedric to set up a leadership team and project operational goals for New Life. Cedric sat in on the final interview meeting with Rev. Thorp and the Fort Collins Board. This meeting would help determine Cedric's involvement beyond June 1.

Cedric began by summarizing the process that had brought Loveland Fellowship to its current status. Then Pastor Houser asked Rev. Thorp and Cedric to discuss personal goals for New Life.

Rev. Thorp noted, "The vision and operation of New Life has primarily come from you, Cedric, correct?"

"Out of the mission to help in flood recovery, the request came from Matt Davidson about a possible church in their vicinity. After such a proposal to the Board of Elders, it was approved. Then Pastor Ethan twisted my arm to become the Bible study leader which I have been for the last eight months."

"What are your plans after June 1 when I assume pastoral leadership?"

"I'm not sure. Regina and I have talked. We want whatever God desires and help New Life succeed. But I don't want to interfere with your plans."

"Operating a church takes multiple gifts to function well, and a new church plant is no different. Perhaps more so. What gifts would you have to offer?" asked Rev. Thorp.

"Administration may be one. I'm an accountant. I have a heart for missions, be it foreign or local. And I'm developing in the area of teaching."

"Each of those three could be valuable to help grow a church. I would ask Rev. Houser's permission to establish a Church Council at New Life to be a team of five to help me grow the church to its maximum capability. I am also asking you to be chairperson of that Council and the Treasurer of the Church."

"I know three couples from Fort Collins Church will need to commit to two years of voluntarily attending and serving at the Loveland Church. Let me talk and pray with my wife before I give you an answer," Cedric offered.

Regina and Cedric transitioned to Loveland Church but continued living near Fort Collins. Along with them, two other families started in June 1978. Cedric became the Treasurer and chairperson of the Church Council. Regina's gift of music filled a massive need for the ministry. Melanie Thorp and Adel Sargent's leadership in women's ministries drew many to the church.

The Weavers contributed their background in children's and youth ministry. These formed the core from which Loveland Fellowship would expand and be a healthy church.

Rev. Thorp's evangelistic gift reached into the Loveland community drawing many to hear and some to adopt faith in Christ. As a result, the church began to grow, so by the anniversary of its first public service, over 150 people attended New Life. The need for more extensive and more practical facilities led them to a large former movie theatre complex. Remodeling included adding multiple rooms for many ministry needs. The congregation celebrated the New Life Loveland Fellowship's grand opening on July 1, 1980, with over 200 people present.

೧ • ೮

Cedric usually was able to make good choices when it came to finances. He was extra cautious when dealing with the church's money. In the fall of 1980, he came across an investment opportunity that might provide personal and church revenue. Based on Cedric's information, the Leadership Team of New Life agreed to invest $10,000 for a promised return of 12% per year. The investment fund's potential led Cedric to draw $40,000 from his retirement savings and place it with the Church's deposit.

The realization that this was a pyramid scheme came about six months later. The arrest of the fund manager alerted investors that their money might be unrecoverable. Cedric believed he had betrayed the church's trust. But the failure to consult Regina before taking their funds was even more shameful. It caused a wedge to work its way into their relationship.

"Cedric, I always trusted you with our finances, but why didn't you tell me first?"

"I made a huge mistake because my money is equally yours. I should have asked you."

"Does Frank Brookstone know what happened?"

"Yes, and he was disappointed but didn't reprimand me," said Cedric.

Cedric did his best to pursue the restoration of funds. Recovery of about 80% of investments returned through civil action five years later. But the immediate response required Cedric to express humble ownership for his actions. He publicly confessed his poor decision to both Loveland and Fort Collins congregations and asked their forgiveness. To Regina, in addition to seeking her forgiveness, he promised a greater degree of financial accountability to rebuild her trust. Both the Church and wife extended their pardon to him.

Cedric prayed, "God, I ask you to forgive me and restore my trustworthiness."

But it was himself that was nearly impossible to forgive. The guilt solidified itself in Cedric's soul. The shame stared back at him when looking in the mirror. The weight continued to build.

Cedric and Regina decided to transition back to the Fort Collins Church. They had given four years of effort to Loveland. They felt their work had been fruitful and effective in training others to take that ministry into the future. They also felt their children, ages eleven and ten, needed involvement at Fort Collins for the next stage in their lives. August of 1982 began a new chapter in the Myer family home.

The return to Fort Collins enabled Cedric to slide back into a less hectic lifestyle. But at the same time, there came that prodding that would not allow comfort to be synonymous with backing away from a divine directive to serve.

"God, what do You mean? Is there a different road You want me to travel?" Cedric prayed.

Being in his thirties made it more challenging for a career change. But Cedric had always been open to change and willing to learn.

Cedric became involved at Fort Collins as the Young Married class teacher. He resonated well with them and became interactive with their home life details. Cedric was concerned with the kind of conflicts that surfaced in their married life. They frequently requested he give counsel to help resolve issues between them. He would usually refer many to Rev. Houser, not feeling trained or qualified.

As he evaluated the number of dissolutions of marriages in Metro Fort Collins and particularly in its churches, he became more interested in ways the church could help. It hit close when a well-respected Elder of Fort Collins Church became a casualty. Few saw it coming, and it appeared irreversible.

As Cedric read more on marriage and divorce, he drew toward those advocating the practical ways of preventing divorce and promoting healthy marriages. It became clear that Christianity's teaching of biblical principles should have a solution. Cedric began exploring ways to help stem the tide of marital failure.

His contact with a leading Divinity School affiliated with the Evangelical Free Church discovered a track for Christian counseling. Cedric began a two-year academic quest to obtain a Marriage and Family Counseling Certificate. He completed the course through a program of videotaped lectures, numerous essays, and exams, receiving his certificate with merit at age thirty-six. Pastor Ethan asked Cedric to make an appointment to discuss some church changes.

"Cedric, I would like to ask you to consider a position with the Fort Collins Church."

"I'm already on the Mission Commission and Sunday School teacher."

"I want you to become an Associate Pastor."

"But I'm not ordained or even licensed. On top of that, you know my struggles with past sins in my life," noted Cedric.

"Why do you still wrestle with sins that God has forgiven you?" asked Pastor Ethan.

"My conscience just keeps reminding me of my imperfections."

"God isn't looking for perfect servants, just sinners saved by grace."

"Well, I'm a sinner that's begged for His grace and wants to serve him."

"I've talked with District Superintendent Dilley and he is giving you a waiver on ordination. And God can use your struggles as an illustration for others to find a God who helps and uses sinners He has forgiven."

Pastor Nathan gave Cedric a few helpful biblical references of such persons whom God has used to build his kingdom.

"What would my duties be?" asked Cedric.

"You would come on the Elder Board, conduct the counseling duties, and assist me in various ministries, even some pulpit supply. I should let you know that I am requesting a three-month sabbatical next summer. You would have more responsibilities while I'm gone."

"What would that mean with my CPA work at Brookstone?"

"While ours is a paid position, it is part-time. You may want to work out an arrangement with Brookstone for consideration of part-time as well."

"Regina and I have a lot to consider. I will get back to you in a week."

A twinge of panic and confusion hit his mind. "Is this what you were preparing me for, God?" asked Cedric.

Regina digested all the information from Cedric. Then she assuredly stated her belief that God was in this request and that her husband would be suitable for the job.

A conference with Frank Brookstone was not immediately as affirming. The demands during tax season made Cedric's absence a bit daunting. But in the end, they came to an agreement allowing for reduced hours to half-time after April 15.

Superintendent Dilley conducted an installation service for Cedric in January of 1984. The hat of pastoral responsibility was more weighty than some others. Yet, it became a gratifying one to wear when he saw God's presence in his work.

Mixed with all his other duties, Cedric took a homiletics crash course. Some included the reading of methods of sermon preparation and delivery. But he gained much from listening to recordings of good preaching like Dr. Jack Hammer. A lot of praying for the Spirit's help was quite advantageous.

However, Cedric did find himself sliding back into a schedule that required making some hard choices. Church versus family responsibilities was a frequent hazard. And too often, the church took priority. Timothy suffered the most from his father's absence from sporting and equestrian events.

"Dad, why can't you come to see me perform at the rodeo with Bandit?"

"I've got a conference to attend that same day," answered Cedric.

"I suppose the church is more important than your son," Tim said sarcastically.

"No, it's not. I'll make it up to you later."

The sting of their conversation left scars for both of them. For Timothy, it brought resentment toward his father and the church. For Cedric, this reminded him that his priorities were out of balance and may become a more significant issue later.

The pastoral duties showed evidence of Cedric's spiritual giftedness. He enjoyed preaching but realized that he was more of a teaching pastor. Though the counseling load was not excessively high, it still consumed his time. Cedric desired pre-marital counseling classes over marriages in trouble. But when the participants of either one were open to God's Word, the returns were gratifying and effective.

"For the Word of God is living and active. Sharper than any double-edge sword, it penetrates even to dividing soul and spirit, joints and marrow; it judges the thoughts and attitudes of the heart." Hebrews 4:12

Reliance on God's Word guarantees one will find the truth. The proclamation of that Word is the duty of those who presume to speak for God. It is in man's best interest to hear and walk in the commands of that Word.

Cedric had not been back to Indiana for over two years. The cap as the oldest child was a respectable one for siblings and a delight to his parents. A trip home in August of 1987 with Regina, Ruth, and Timothy was a time of reunion and a reminder of how time changes people.

Dad showed signs of aging with graying hair and a slight backbend when walking. With Willis now managing it, the shop thrived, and Dad focused more on car sales.

"So mom, I hear you got promoted to charge nurse in the Pediatrics ward. How do you like it?

"I always liked working with kids, and I try to get their minds off their pain."

"So, do you make more than Dad?" Cedric asked probingly.

"Most months I do unless he sells a couple of Cadillacs," she said with a twinkle.

Following graduation in 1974, Willis had taken an intensive mechanics trade course. He continued learning on the job under Dad's tutelage before becoming head mechanic in 1978. Willis had married Candice Miller in 1976.

"Hey Willis," Cedric hollered, "How many children do you have now?

"We've got three boys and two girls," responded Willis, "and that's in 9 years."

"Well, you must not spend all your time down at the shop."

Dorinda married Mark Threadgood, a construction worker. In 1973 they moved to a Native American reservation to assist a missions outreach. This setting was perfect for Dorinda. Her art captured the unique beauty of the southwest desert and its culture. Before moving back to the Midwest in 1985, they would have three boys to raise, each given Indian middle names.

Rowena finished high school in 1971 then put her dreams to flight. She was trained and hired by United Airlines as a stewardess. She traveled the world for the next ten years. In 1981 she met and married Brad Nussbaum, a pilot with United Airlines.

"Brad, how did you and Rowena meet?" asked Regina.

"We were on the same flight crew that flew to Germany in 1979."

"So what made her give up her wings and settle down in Naperville?"

"An emergency landing in Barcelona with one engine fixed her traveling quest."

God granted them a daughter in 1982 and adopted another daughter from Korea in 1984. They chose to live in Naperville to be close to the United hub at O'Hare.

Then there was Willow. She continued honing her dancing skills and convinced Mom and Dad to let her take dance training classes starting at sixth grade. Her auditions led to selections by high school music directors and community theater. Her talent became well known and, in 1975, entered Julliard's School of Ballet. Throughout the 1980's she toured and starred with the New York Metropolitan Ballet Troupe. Big brother would follow her career and numerous times surprise her by being in the audience of her performances.

The decade of Cedric's thirties was full of bountiful blessings. The various roles in life were significant in defining who he was. While the church ministry appeared to take center stage, Cedric valued life with his immediate family most. He was learning how to apportion each to their rightful place.

CHAPTER 5

The Sunroom

"There is a time for everything, and a season for every activity under heaven." Ecclesiastes 3:1

There are multiple reasons for installing additions to a house. Most do it for needed space. But for others, it is a means of having a different kind of room. Such is the case with the "sunroom." This area allows for enjoying a panoramic view of the outdoors and allows light to shine indoors. With adaptation, it is a functional place for all seasons of life.

Upon entering his forties, Cedric prepared himself to share his marriage insights with a broader audience. Being on the pastoral staff at Fort Collins allowed him to practice the art of public speaking and providing counsel. His ministry there had been received well by many. Now he was ready to test if more churches and pastors might desire his ministry gifts.

Cedric designed one-day seminars and two-day retreat formats. He also offered a Sunday sermon option for pulpit supply. A synopsis of these offerings was printed on a three-leaf flyer and sent to all Evangelical Free churches in Colorado. He also sent copies to Superintendent Dilley for possible distribution.

Regina and Cedric sat in their sunroom to discuss this outreach ministry. They wanted to establish parameters to make this venture workable for their family and recipients.

"I think we should place a limit of conducting only one weekend retreat per month while the children live at home," proposed Regina.

Cedric suggested, "Whenever possible, a family member should travel with me for company and accountability."

"I think that would be great for you and the kids. Perhaps you could find duties for them as assistants in conducting the seminars," added Regina.

"Perhaps you could join me to share ideas from a wife's perspective."

"Oh, I have a few opinions and suggestions to give," she said with a smile.

"What do you think, honey, of donating all proceeds beyond expenses incurred to some other worthy ministry?"

"I believe that would be honorable to God and not self-serving," said Regina.

Cedric had no real expectation of what the response might be. He was pretty surprised upon receiving six inquiries the first month. To him, it was a sign that there was a great need for such ministry. It certainly wasn't a matter of his popularity. Nor did he want it to be.

The first engagement was at New Life Loveland Fellowship. The pastor scheduled a one-day seminar for Saturday, July 16, 1988. Forty couples signed up to attend. It was a joy to return to this congregation, meet old friends, and make new ones. Matt Davidson expressed gratitude for their partnership in establishing New Life Church and seeing its growth.

"Can you believe that we have over 250 attendees now?" said Matt.

"Especially when you think we started with ten in your living room," replied Cedric.

"We were only a mustard seed group, but God gave the increase."

"Keep the faith, Matt. He's isn't done yet."

A Boulder pastor arranged for a weekend retreat for August 19-21. The setting for this event was YMCA-R in Estes Park. Cedric looked forward to returning to his former residence when coming to Colorado. The Myer family reserved a cabin, and Dad showed Ruth and Tim his former home.

As they unpacked, Jay, his old friend, poked his head into the cabin door.

"Well, look at you. What are you still doing here at YMCA?" asked Cedric.

"If you stay long enough, they'll move you up. I'm head of the Maintenance Dept."

"Regina, this guy was the one with me when we saw you at the rodeo in '69."

"I'm happy to meet you. You brought me the prize," replied Regina.

"He never clued me in till after we got back to Estes Park," said Jay.

"We'll be here for the weekend," noted Cedric. "Stick your head into the meeting room and hear me."

"I might just do that. At least I'll try seeing you again before you leave."

The retreat schedule included one session on Friday night, four on Saturday, and a Sunday morning worship service where Cedric preached. Built-in breaks gave couples time to discuss issues from these sessions alone. This freedom allowed some to walk Rocky Mountain National Park paths for their alone time.

The 70 couples expressed mostly favorable responses to the sessions' content on their evaluations. A few people indicated a need to work on their spouse's concerns. But one pair stated that their marriage was in serious trouble. Cedric felt helpless with no name or contact option except to pray for them. From this, he modified the closing challenge to future seminar attendees, encouraging them to seek help from a trusted counselor.

This weekend in Estes Park was to be a bonding time for the Myer family. Even though Dad worked, he reserved time between sessions for Ruth, Tim, and Regina. The kids were now seventeen and sixteen years of age. They weren't the most thrilled to be away from their friends and stuck in a cabin with mom and dad at this stage of life.

"I could be at the ranch practicing my calf roping with Bandit," grumbled Timothy.

"What's there to do here with a bunch of adults in meetings," complained Ruth.

"There will be a long break on Saturday afternoon, and I hoped we could climb up Fall River Road in the Land Rover. The one-lane dirt passage to the Alpine Visitor Center will be adventurous and scenic," dad said.

As an added incentive, each child selected the restaurant of their choice in Estes Park. Ruth picked the Pink Lady Café for Sunday dinner, and Tim chose The Stable for their Saturday night meal. In addition, Regina took both kids trail riding Saturday AM during retreat sessions.

The most significant benefit was time together as a family. It became more elusive as the children got older and had other social choices. Cedric realized that the kids were entering adulthood and would not be living with him and Regina in the not-too-distant future.

"A time to weep and a time to laugh"
Ecclesiastes 3:4a

One-on-one moments with one's children are few but invaluable. In 1989, Ruth traveled with her dad to a Colorado Springs seminar, providing father and daughter time to talk.

"Dad, what was it about Mom that made you want her to marry you."

"Besides being a hot babe, her humility and kind heart drew me."

"Was it love at first sight?"

"It was a "like at first sight" for me. And love for her was my choice."

"I hope I find a man like you to be my husband."

"I hope you get even better, hon."

Ruth would graduate that year. She, like her mother, had accepted her purity ring at a banquet for mid-teen girls of Fort Collins Church. Tearfully, Cedric prayed for his daughter and future husband.

Regina and Cedric were quite pleased that Ruth chose Denver Bible College. Dropping her off was a lump in your throat moment. But they knew she was ready to be on her own and they had confidence in the College's priorities in preparing their students to be of service to God. Besides, she wasn't all that far away to allow visits in either direction.

Fewer father and son times availed themselves. However, one of the most memorable times came on a fall afternoon. Cedric lit the fireplace, and they took popcorn and drinks of choice into the sunroom. A Navy/Airforce football game was on TV. Of course, Timothy was for the Airforce and Dad for the Navy. Most of the conversation was football-related. But during half-time, Cedric asked Timothy some key questions.

"What do you think you want to do after high school, Tim?"

"I might become a mechanic or work for Grandpa on the ranch."

"Do you see that as a career plan for the rest of your life?" asked Cedric.

"I like both, and you can make a good living with them."

"They're both noble professions, and I just want you to be successful and satisfied."

"Maybe I'll join the Airforce on a football scholarship," Tim said in jest.

The requests kept coming for Cedric's seminars and speaking engagements. Some even came from other states. To tie in a trip to see his parents in Indiana, he contacted his boyhood home church to consider a single service opportunity. They asked for a one-day seminar and a Sunday morning sermon. Cedric agreed.

They scheduled the third weekend of July 1990 for the trip. Ruth had completed her first year in college but traveled to see grandma and grandpa Myer with the family. Timothy was delighted to help do some driving, especially on the four-lane roads. Regina didn't relish the twenty-four hour one-way travel times but was anxious to see Cedric's family.

Except for Willow, all the siblings, nephews, and nieces managed to gather at Mom and Dad's house for an old-fashioned pig roast meal. The whole family had a rollicking good time. It was heart-warming to see the maturity in each of the siblings. Observing the growing Myer family was equally rewarding.

"A time to kill and a time to heal"
Ecclesiastes 3:3a

While at Dad Myer's house, a call came for Cedric on Friday afternoon. It was Bob. Cedric's mind rushed back twenty-three years. What does he say to his former best friend? Even though no hatred lingered, some pain did.

"Hi, Cedric. I was wondering if we could meet somewhere to talk?"

"I guess we could. Where and when?"

"How about on the lot where the old mill used to stand? Is 3:00 OK?"

"That will work. See you."

Both knew that their conversation would be awkward and perhaps challenging. Twenty years allow for a lot of changes to occur in life and one's attitudes. Bob had inquired several times about Cedric from Willis; Cedric had not asked anyone about Bob.

"Glad to see you again, Rick," Bob stated.

"It's been a long time. How are things with you?"

"Well, they definitely could be better," Bob said nervously. "Cedric, I'm so sorry for what happened between us."

"I am too. Are you and Carma married?"

"No. We dated for six months and found out she was pregnant."

"So you and she have a child. Is it a boy or girl?" asked Cedric.

"We don't have a child. She left for the east coast and got an abortion. After that, she moved to Oklahoma to be with an older sister. A year later, she committed suicide."

"What made her do that, Bob? Did her sister say what happened?"

"I heard that she just could never get over the loss of the baby and felt hopeless."

"O Bob, how sad and tragic So what have you done? Are you with anyone now?"

"Monica and I eventually got back together. But it's a love, hate marriage. We fight all the time, and she holds it over me that I left her for Carma."

Suddenly, a rush of compassion came into Cedric. He felt sorry for Bob and his loveless union with Monica. He sensed pity for Carma for a life shattered and without hope, wondering if he had not rejected her desires that she might still be alive. To all this was added a thankfulness for Regina's companionship and love.

Cedric knew that only Christ Jesus could bring Bob out of this pit. Only God could heal the mess of a marriage he and Monica had. So he asked Bob to consider coming to both Saturday's seminar and Sunday's service.

"I don't know if Monica would come. We haven't been to church forever."

"Tell her I share in her pain, but I invite her to come."

Monica and Bob sat as far to the auditorium's rear as possible. Her facial expressions at first were hardened and down-looking. But as the day progressed, Cedric began noticing some interest, and she looked straight at him. Cedric rushed back and put his arm around Monica.

"Thank you for coming. There is hope for you and Bob. Please come tomorrow for the morning service, and I'll share how to see that hope realized."

"Ok, I'll be here," Monica promised.

On Sunday, Bob and Monica were present for the service. Cedric used Hosea and Gomer's story to show how the love of God illustrated the desire to bring healing to troubled marriages. And how forgiveness was the path to that wholeness. At the altar call, Monica and Bob stood to express their desire for God's forgiveness and a willingness for marital restoration.

Before heading back to Colorado, Cedric and Bob met again.

"Bob, I forgive you and want to restore our friendship."

"I have missed it a lot. Let's stay in touch."

"I've asked the pastor here to take you under his care and give you counsel."

"Monica and I will do our best to work out our differences. Thanks Rick."

Cedric was never as exhausted for a trip home as now. But he was also never as happy either. Cedric and Regina relinquished themselves to the back seat with Tim driving and Ruth next to him.

Looking over at Regina, Cedric whispered, "I love you," and squeezed her hand.

Ruth returned to the Denver Bible college in September. Each student selected a three-month community service time as part of their degree requirement. It needed to relate to some humanitarian need. Ruth chose to assist in a young women's shelter for girls rescued from abusive homes or who had been in sex trafficking. Her compassionate heart became a magnet to women who felt unloved.

"A time for war and a time for peace."
Ecclesiastes 3:8b)

Timothy did a significant turnaround with his academic endeavors. His GPA was 3.8 when he graduated. In his Junior year, he decided to apply for admission to the Air Force Academy in Colorado Springs. It took many discussions to obtain his mother's approval, but she gave her blessing to Timothy's wishes in the end. It required a minimum of nine years' commitment to the US Air Force. His parents signed a letter of consent for his admission.

"A time to embrace and a time to refrain"
Ecclesiastes 3:5b

In the fall of 1991, Regina and Cedric entered the empty nest stage in their marriage. A quiet home has its appeal, but the silence can also be deafening.

Regina reflected, "I miss the kid's chatter and just their presence."

"We hoped that they would become adults. Leaving is part of that," replied Cedric.

"So what do we do with all our extra time?"

"You could learn how to knit booties for your future grandchildren."

"Grandchildren? They're not even married yet."

"Thought you might be a slow learner," suggested Cedric as he laughed.

Regina decided that she would enjoy returning to the dental hygienist work. Her former employer was quite ready to add her to the staff. The worship and music role at Fort Collins EFC also provided an outlet for her gifts and talents.

Cedric never made claims that his marriage to Regina was perfect. He would illustrate conflicts and resolutions from their union in his seminars. Though never abusive nor intentionally demeaning, there had been differences that required both to learn proper communication techniques. They realized that neither one was always right. Cedric became smart in learning when to defend and when to back off. He wasn't one to pick a fight.

"A time to be silent and a time to speak"
Ecclesiastes 3:7b

Cedric accepted a new position in 1992. District Superintendent Dilley asked him to serve on the Conference Pastor's Licensing Board. This board examined the candidate's qualification for affiliation with the Evangelical Free Church. They usually would meet quarterly, depending on the need. Because it was often a subjective call, approving a man's right to preach, lead and oversee God's flock was a serious matter. Some men should not receive a license due to capability or character issues.

Ruth graduated with a degree in Social Relations on May 25, 1993. She took a position at the women's shelter of Denver.

On Christmas of 1992, Ruth introduced the family to Andrew Reese. He was a handsome gentleman, and it was apparent they were deeply in love. In October, they were married. Andrew was a Youth Pastor at a large church in Denver. He had been a year ahead of Ruth in Bible College. Cedric walked a "mile" down the aisle of Fort Collins Church to hand his daughter to her waiting love.

Timothy completed his training at the Academy on June 3, 1995. He received commissioning as an officer in the USAF as a radar specialist. It was a proud moment for the family,who witnessed Tim's pinning in his blue parade uniform. His first orders were to a California base for additional training before being stationed in Japan.

Before leaving for California, Ruth and Timothy planned a surprise twenty-fifth-anniversary party for their parents with Grandma and Grandpa Murphy's help. The event took place on June 10. An invitation to the party went to the Myer family in Indiana, but only Mom and Dad could attend. Celebrating at the ranch provided an apropos site for Regina and Cedric.

Cedric and Regina had purchased tickets for a trip to Hawaii. The plane left on June 17 for a two-week land and cruise vacation that included a vow renewal ceremony aboard a ship.

"If you had it to do over again, would you marry me?" asked Regina.

"You had me over a barrel then. I didn't have much choice."

"So what's different now? Am I less alluring?

"You're even more attractive to me. I'd marry you any day. After all, we are on our second honeymoon," Cedric said.

Life for the Myers family was at a very fulfilling point. The marriage seminars continued to expand, their jobs went well, and the family remained cohesive. It was hard to imagine it being much better.

"A time to be born and a time to die"
Ecclesiastes 3:2a

Carl Murphy, family patriarch, church elder, and rancher, was reported missing on February 24, 1997. As president of the Western Cattle Ranchers Association, he attended a Cheyenne, WY meeting. A private plane was flying him home when it disappeared over northern Colorado. The following day the wreckage was found in a mountainous area.

It was a tragic loss for many. Janice was hard to console, as was Regina. But Timothy received the news with great distress for the loss of his close confidant. Carl was able to relate with Tim better than anyone else. He was allowed to fly home from Japan for the memorial service. Together the family grieved and searched for purpose in this accident.

The sun room allows for inner protection and grace for all "times." Spring, Summer, Fall, and Winter each have their extremes. But despite them, one can usually depend on the comforting rays from the SON to bring hope.

CHAPTER 6

Reconstructing

"Therefore we do not lose heart. Though outwardly we are wasting away, yet inwardly we are being renewed day by day."
II Corinthians 4:16

Houses, at times, face traumatic forces of nature. From floods, earthquakes, fire, tornadoes to hurricanes. Often, the beginnings of these storms are small clouds that become ominous, catching their occupants off-guard.

So also, homes and their families may get caught in destructive relationship storms. Seeds of discontent, neglect and unchecked words subtly planted when nurtured become a violent fury of emotions. To reconstruct can take significant effort and time.

This decade was to be the most challenging and change-filled period for the Myer family. While there would be numerous delights, there would also be painful experiences. Surviving and being able to find the good would require some significant reconstructing of lives and relationships.

Life sometimes forces changes that are beyond one's control. So it was with the death of Carl. The church needed to install a new elder. The Cattle Ranch Association elected a different president. And Janice Murphy was facing the daunting task of running a home and business without Carl's guidance. She came to understand how much she relied on him.

Red Parsons stepped up to manage the cattle's care with the help of Rex and Duely. Janice also leaned on the advice of friend and neighbor rancher Clyde. 700 head of cattle was a huge responsibility to oversee. The winter feeding alone was a gigantic process to get hay and water to these grazing machines.

By the Spring of 1998, Janice had adapted to widowhood and its realities. But the scope of work and decision-making seemed overwhelming. She asked Regina and Cedric to discuss her future.

"I'm 72, and the ranch is a big load on my shoulders. I want your help."

"What would you like us to do for you, Mom?"

"This ranch has been my home for fifty years. And I consider it a blessing. But when I'm gone, this will all be yours. Whatever we do, I feel you should have input."

"I hadn't given that a lot of consideration. Have you thought of what you want," asked Regina?

"The house without your dad is too big. Maybe I should move to a retirement village in town."

Cedric spoke up, "Mom, I'd hate to see you give up the place. It's your home."

"I know its my home, but it just isn't the same without Carl. Red and the ranch hands are doing a great job, but making decisions regarding the cattle is more than I want to care for," said Janice.

"Let us give it some thought and ask for divine wisdom," Regina suggested.

Cedric and Regina said their goodbyes and headed home. Regina was quiet as they drove from the ranch. She, too, was weighing the scope of taking on such an enterprise. They spent the evening and into the night talking.

"Our first responsibility is to help Mom. I know she's lonely," said Regina

"What if we were to move to the ranch?" Cedric asked.

"Where would Mom go?"

"We could build an on-suite for her at the back of the house."

"That would certainly end her living alone. I think it's worth suggesting. What about the cattle? Red isn't young anymore."

"We need to talk about that with your mom. It might be time for more changes," said Cedric.

"I know I need your help, especially with financial decisions," Regina added.

Janice was pleasantly surprised but delighted about them moving to the ranch. It meant she could stay on the farm and not have to care for everything alone. By late fall with the on-suite completed, Janice moved her items. Cedric and Regina remodeled the master bedroom, then moved to the ranch in November. They decided to hold off selling their house for the moment.

In consultation with Red, Clyde, and the Western Cattle Ranchers Association's current president, Cedric suggested a slow but steady sell-off of the cattle. Janice and Regina agreed.

Over the next three years, the herd went from 700 to twenty-five. The sale produced operating capital, provided investments, and reduced workers' needed.

Changes were also taking place at the Fort Collins Church. Cedric had resigned from his position as Associate Pastor at the beginning of 1998. Rev. Houser announced his retirement on March 17, 1999. A three-month search resulted in Rev. Standish coming from Houston, TX, with his wife and two teenage sons.

A growing church with 275 people needed more pastoral staff. Rev. Standish evaluated the needs of the congregation and community. He proposed the church hire a youth and children's pastor. After conducting interviews, Pastor Andrew Reese came on staff. Cedric and Regina were excited to have Ruth's family near them. Andrew and expectant Ruth moved into the old Myer house. Regina received a call on May 8, 2000

"It's a girl," Andrew said excitedly.

"Give us all the details!"

"Carletta Marie is short, fat, and loud," Andrew replied.

"I meant inches, pounds, and color of hair," Regina quipped. "Wait till I tell grandpa."

Grandpa, Cedric thought, now that is a change. He felt both elated and old. The house needed baby protection. Diaper changing would return. But the idea of holding his grandchild was heartwarming.

Cedric answered his phone on a Friday afternoon in June 2001.

"Hello, Cedric speaking. How can I help you."

"Could you bring me a U-Haul?" said the voice on the other end?

"Is this Tim? If it is, that might take a while to get across the Pacific."

"Yes, I wanted to let you know that I'm transferring."

"To where?"

"To a NORAD base in the States."

"Well, which state?"

"A base in Colorado Springs, the Peterson AF Base."

"That's super, Tim. When will you be here?"

"July 15th. And dad, there's something more. I'm bringing someone with me."

"Who is it?"

"My wife, Yoko. We were married last month."

Cedric tried his best not to let his disappointment come across the phone. Not because Yoko was Japanese, but because Tim hadn't informed his parents of the wedding earlier. Cedric felt that perhaps he was not as communicative with his son as a father should be.

"We promise to get to Colorado Springs as soon as you arrive to welcome you both."

Regina could not wait long and called her son to tell him she would have loved to be at their wedding.

"I love you, son," said Regina, "and I look forward to seeing you and Yoko soon."

Ruth brought Carletta to the house almost weekly. Of course, Grandma and Great-grandma doted on her. But it was always special when she got to sit in Grandpa's lap and get tickled. Her favorite thing was when Cedric bounced her on his knee. She was conditioning to ride a horse in the not-so-distant future.

After Timothy arrived at the NORAD base, Regina asked him and Yoko to spend a weekend at the ranch. The Paradise Retreat guest house was ideal for lodging them. It had been five years since Tim had been home. It was somewhat painful as he reminisced about Carl and shared stories of his grandpa with Yoko. Yoko's broken English did not interfere in their conversations, and the family became endeared to her.

Following paring down the cattle to twenty-five, Regina, Janice, and Cedric discussed the ranch's use.

"Mom, we don't need 2,500 acres anymore."

"Do you think we should sell it?" asked Janice.

"No," said Regina, "but perhaps we could lease 2,000 of it to another rancher."

"That would still leave enough land to feed a few cattle and the horses," Cedric added.

"We can still do a lot on 500 acres," reasoned Janice.

"Cedric and I have been talking about a possible ministry use for the rest."

"What did you have in mind?"

Cedric replied, "One idea we had was a small camping area with a few cabins and maybe RV sites."

"It could provide a site for Cedric's marriage retreats, youth outings, and family camps," added Regina.

"I like that suggestion! It would be a great tribute to Carl," Janice noted happily.

"Let me check out the county regulations, put together a site plan, and obtain some cost projections," said Cedric.

In the fall, acceptance came for a non-profit camping ministry concept by the "Carl and Janice Trust dated January 10, 1949". The Ministry was named Mount Eden Camp. The passing of the State's site plans, granting building permits, and ordering cabin kits for Spring delivery paved the way for construction.

The funds for Mount Eden came from leasing the land to a neighboring rancher and the sale of cattle. The eight cabins, a meeting lodge, and seven RV hookup sites provided enough space for fifty people. The place was in a clearing behind and above the barn.

On the Sunday afternoon before Thanksgiving 2001, Rev. Standish conducted a service of dedication and celebration. Invitations went to Fort Collins friends of the Myers and Murphy family to designate Mount Eden Camp as a ministry for God's use. About seventy-five people were in attendance

Fort Collins Church youth group became the first retreat at Mount Eden. Andrew and Ruth were retreat leaders. Regina had secured a dozen trail horses, using them in many camp outings. Ranch hand Rex was the one who oversaw and usually led the rides.

About a quarter of Mount Eden Camp was Marriage and Family-related in the summer. Through Ruth's contacts with the young women's shelter, one week each year was reserved to provide ministry to their residents. Occasionally a furloughed missionary family or retired pastors made use of the facilities. These ministries would have blessed Carl.

The Myer family came to realize that life is not always joy without sorrow. Death brought some painful losses. In February of 2002, Regina found Mother Murphy deceased, having died peacefully in her sleep.

Cedric's parents passing came a year apart from each other. His mother had undergone treatment for bladder cancer for several years. Mom Myer went to her eternal home in October of 2003. The following July, a call came from Willis.

"Cedric, Dad had a massive heart attack. He died on the spot at the shop."

Home-going had a dual meaning for Cedric those two years. Willis and Dorinda carried a lot of the weight in planning the arrangements. All the sibs and spouses were able to make the memorial services.

Two births in 2005 countered these losses. Reginald Tobishi Myer, Timothy and Yoko's son, made his debut on September 11. His cousin Allen Lee Myer came on November 4 at Fort Collins Memorial to Andrew and Ruth Reese. Born with a cleft palate required numerous surgeries in the years ahead. It was joy and consolation amid pain as parents and grandparents observed their child suffering.

Cedric realized that birth and death are opposite ends of life. In time both are to be experienced by families. Their subtraction and addition reconstruct the family.

As Cedric entered his fifties, he recognized several changes within himself. He was a little less agile than at age twenty-five. His favorite clothes were usually old outfits worn for years. The same foods ended up on his plate. And the guy in the mirror had become more wrinkled.

In her late forties and early fifties, Regina began experiencing discomforting changes in her menstrual cycle. It caused more than the traditional hot flashes of menopause.

With it came dramatic mood swings that often left her feeling lethargic or depressed. Some weeks saw her remain in bed for most of several days. Her self-esteem lowered and making her quite tense and irritable. In one instance, Cedric tried to light-heartedly jest with her, but it backfired.

"Where did that gray hair on top of your head come from, Regina?

"So you think I'm getting old, do you?" she replied sarcastically.

"No, you look ravishing, my dear."

"All I ravish anymore is the refrigerator.

"You're barely over a hundred pounds," assured Cedric.

"Maybe an ugly hundred pounds,"

A trip to the hair salon provided a cosmetic correction in her follicle malfunction. Regina was not vain, but she saw no harm in adjusting nature's time plan. She maintained this process for about six months then finally accepted the truth. Cedric took her to a spa sitting for some Glamor Shots emphasizing her beauty.

Before she died, Janice recognized the signs of her daughter's struggles and suggested she consult an OBGYN doctor. Cedric, perplexed at first, agreed and accompanied her to the office of Dr. Paterson. With the help of prescribed medicines, adjusted and monitored for several years, Regina slowly reduced the severity of her symptoms. Some dietary restrictions and modifications also helped lessen the discomforts. And by her late fifties, she was almost free of them.

Though Cedric had declined many marriage seminars in 2001, the pace picked back up through 2007. More frequent requests came by couples asking for private counseling sessions. Usually, these sessions lasted for months to a year before there were signs of change. More intense counseling involved the partners staying at Paradise Retreat over a weekend. The approach brought restoration to most of those who came, but not all.

Personally, Cedric continued wrestling more frequently with the guilt and shame of past mistakes. The advent of the internet led him to allow his curiosity to open some sites of sexually-explicit nature. The realization that he had likely crossed the same line as his father led to even more self-condemnation.

Despite his professed faith and ministry successes, he continued to carry his "old bag of sins" as a daily reminder of his imperfections and precarious position with God. As time progressed, these weights led to a feeling of hypocrisy. His busy schedule crowded out time for meditation and prayer. And he caught himself getting short with Regina and less open to her.

"Regina, why isn't dinner ready? You know I've got a meeting tonight."

"You've always got a meeting or seminar to conduct," retorted Regina.

"Don't you look at the calendar?"

"You could have reminded me this morning!"

Cedric buried himself deeper into his work to compensate for feelings of inadequacies as a Christian and husband. He scheduled more seminars and retreats that would take him away from home. In turn, this left Regina feeling lonely and unsupported. She also spent more hours at the dental clinic.

Little by little, their marriage began showing the strains of each one's separation. Their intimacies became an act of duty and passionless. Though attempting to disguise them, anger and frustration pervaded their attitude toward each other. A storm was brewing.

When Cedric was home, Regina planned events that would allow her to be gone. So it was not a total surprise when she approached Cedric in June of 2007.

"I need to get away privately. A friend invited me to their cabin in Canon City. I leave Friday and will get back on Sunday afternoon."

"Well, I'm speaking at a church in Pueblo Sunday morning anyway," Cedric stated.

"I guess that will give us both something to do."

Regina left mid-morning Friday. Cedric busied himself with preparations for Sunday.

While working at the desk, he stumbled upon a dental clinic memo at the bottom of the waste can.

Opening it, he read, "Can't wait for our getaway this weekend, Jim."

The only Jim he knew was a new colleague of Regina's at the dental clinic. He read it several times, trying to make sense of it all. There was disbelief that his wife would violate her vows and marriage by being unfaithful. But reality set in as he fell to his knees.

"Regina, Regina, please don't do this. Don't throw away everything dear to you."

The heartache he felt was ten times more devastating than with Carma's letter. Sobs gushed out of his throat as he considered the demise of his marriage. He lay weeping for almost an hour.

Finally, he pulled himself together. Going to the barn, he pulled out the Rover. His anger had him consider heading for Canon City. Instead, he drove to the top of the hill toward the mountain. Looking down, he saw the farm, Paradise Retreat, Camp Eden, and the house. The many happy memories he had shared with Regina might be a thing of the past.

For a fleeting moment, the thought of ending it all raced through his mind. But he knew he didn't want to meet God that way. He was desperate for answers. He heard a gentle voice.

"Why won't you trust Me with this?" He realized what the source of the voice was.

"Dear God, I need you so much. Please forgive...please forgive...."

Cedric couldn't finish his request. He wanted to say, "forgive Regina," but knew it was himself that needed forgiving. So many times, he had asked God, and the transgressions still clung to is soul. Why ask again?

As he headed back toward the barn and stored the Rover, confusion filled his thoughts. He tried not to think of the probable scenario of what was taking place in Canon City. What would his reactions be when Regina returned? He didn't know.

He first called the pastor of the church he was scheduled to speak at.

"Rev. Stevens, I regret that I must cancel my speaking engagement this Sunday. There's been a family emergency."

"Sorry to hear that Cedric, we will be praying for your family."

"Please do. I'm sorry for the inconvenience."

Secondly, something had him pull down a videotape of a sermon by Dr. Jack Hammer, entitled, "The Grace In Forgiveness." From it, he wrote down three impacting statements."

"Forgiveness means to release or let go. Failure to let go of our sins when given to God negates his grace."

"If we want his grace, then we must forgive others who have hurt us just like he has forgiven us."

"Forgiving grace will heal the damage sins have caused."

After hearing and meditating on this message, Cedric fell prostrate on the floor before God. He envisioned his bag of sins he had been dragging with him through life. He imagined God taking that bag and throwing it into the "sea of forgetfulness." And he prayed:

"God, thank you for your forgiveness of all my sins, helping me let them go. And God, forgive me for hurting Regina. I, in return, forgive her in advance no matter what. Help me show her, your grace."

There was instantly a miraculous peace that covered Cedric's heart, mind, and soul. He had peace with his Savior. And his heart filled with unconditional love for Regina. Retiring, he slept for the next eight hours, waking rested.

On Saturday, he spent the day first cleaning the house thoroughly. The local florist delivered two bouquets, placing one on the dining room table and another on Regina's nightstand. A handwritten letter of love was composed through the afternoon. It took the sixth draft before he finally had satisfaction in what he wanted to convey.

Knowing her plans were to be home Sunday but not knowing the exact time, Cedric spent the day reading God's Word and praying to Him. He also played endless songs of praise and worship, with a few favorite love songs. He countered every evil thought about Regina by listing reasons for loving her.

At 6:30 PM, he heard her car pull up to the house. Regina sat for several minutes, dreading to go in and meet Cedric. Tears of sorrow flowed from her eyes as she anticipated yet another ugly confrontation. Finally, she entered the front door.

Standing in front of her was Cedric. He slowly held up the note from Jim for her to see that he knew.

She gasped in horror, "You found the note."

She then watched as Cedric tore the note into unreadable pieces, placing them in the wastebasket.

"What note?" Cedric said softly and kindly.

With that, Regina broke down and wept uncontrollably. Cedric wrapped his arms around her and held her for several minutes. Then he led her to the couch and sat next to her.

"I never went to Canon City. I stayed alone in a Colorado Springs motel, crying and sleeping. I'm so sorry, Cedric."

As they sat, Regina confessed how the relationship with Jim started and why she cut it off. "It was an emotional affair, but I never had sex with him. I couldn't get the image of the purity ring out of my mind."

Cedric reassured her of his love and total forgiveness. He explained his coming to terms with the shame and guilt for his past. Then he asked her forgiveness for not being the husband she needed. He presented her his letter of love.

With the kind of damage storms cause, naturally and in relationships, it takes time to reconstruct. Regina and Cedric attended a marriage rekindling seminar as participants, not facilitators. He began cutting his retreat and seminar schedule drastically to be available for Regina. Weekly dates were established. And they started and ended each day praying for the other. The restored marriage had more profound strength than the original, in time.

CHAPTER 7

Maintenance

A law of thermodynamics holds that everything is in a state of decay. Given time, everything eventually falls apart. So, without intervention, houses, cars, and even people disintegrate. Maintenance is one form of intervention. It is an attempt to restore or repair that which is decaying.

Cedric's 1957 Chevy serviced him well for many years. Frequently he needed to have a mechanic or the body repair shop intervene when parts wore out, or rust surfaced. To make it last longer, he stored his prize vehicle during winters to delay the inevitable.

Cedric had not forgotten his promise to Bob. He invited him and Monica to a week at the ranch with a plan of showing them the Rockies. An ulterior motive was to check on the health of their marriage. They came in the summer of 2009, giving Cedric and Bob opportunity to strengthen their friendship. There was also an improvement in Bob's marriage to Monica.

In late July, an exciting call came to Cedric from Willow. She was flying to Denver for a business meeting and wanted to see him.

"How long will you be able to stay with us, Willow?"

"My meeting is on Monday and might last all day. I could then stay for several days after that."

"Super, sis, we will have space for you to stay with us."

"Could you pick me up that Monday after the meeting?"

"Yes, just let me know when you get in."

Willow's visit was an excellent time to catch up on each other's lives.

"Well, I got canned from the ballet troupe. Fifty was a little too old."

"I'm sorry, Willow, what are you going to do now?" Cedric asked.

"Don't worry. I've set up my own dance company in Los Angeles."

"Why LA? That's a long way from New York."

"My goal is to become a choreographer for movie producers, and that makes LA more advantageous."

"You are quite the entrepreneur. I wish you great success. Any thought of getting married?"

"It might be too difficult to manage both. I enjoy the single life."

Her contact spurred Cedric to reconnect with his other siblings. A conference for Christian counselors in Chicago allowed him to meet Rowena for lunch at the Palmer House Restaurant.

"With Mom and Dad both gone, we don't see each other as often," Rowena stated.

"Especially since we have scattered all over the country."

"I heard you had Willow at your place, and she's moved to LA."

"Maybe we'll see her name in the movie credits someday."

Cedric asked Willis to order him a good condition late model Prius. Willis found a 2010 black four-door and delivered it himself to his brother.

"The Prius sure lived up to its gas economy marketing on the way out," said Willis.

"That was the main reason I wanted it, plus with the good resale value," replied Cedric.

"You'll probably get a little less here in the mountains."

"That's okay. It will do much better than the Rover," Cedric noted.

A few extra days together gave Willis time to see the reason Cedric stayed in Colorado. Cedric took Willis up Pikes Peak, down into the Royal Gorge, and the panoramic views of Rocky Mountain Park.

"They don't have scenes like this back in Indiana," said Cedric.

"No, they don't. I'll have to come back here more."

"You will always be welcome, brother,"

Willis chose to take the California Zephyr train back to Indiana out of Denver. Rail travel gave him a more relaxed chance to see the plains states in the middle of the USA. The train's night travel granted him some sleep before returning to work in his shop.

Contact with Timothy in Colorado Springs had been sporadic, mainly due to Tim's rigid schedule. Reginald's birth, however, brought more frequent visits in both directions. Grandma Myer looked for any excuse to see her namesake. And Yoko became more comfortable traveling with Reggie to the ranch by herself.

Timothy's faith practices had suffered since joining the USAF. He believed in God but had shelved regular attendance at a church. Yoko, who was not a Christian, led him to avoid it altogether. At six foot three, he liked playing basketball at a local Gym. He became friends with several regulars, particularly with an older player known as Dr. Paul. They, along with Luke, liked to scrimmage three on three as a team against other men.

Dr. Paul gained Timothy's trust to the point of sharing his faith with him. After about a year of conversations with each other, Dr. Paul challenged Tim to rededicate his life to Christ. Only then did Dr. Paul share his vocation as a radio personality at an organization aiming to help families. Yoko, seeing a more loving and tender nature in her husband, also became a Christ-follower. They began attending Dr. Paul's church regularly. Timothy accepted Dr. Paul's offer to mentor him for the following year. You might say this was heart repair.

Restore to me the joy of your salvation and grant me
a willing spirit to sustain me." Psalm 51:12

Cedric and Regina had been aware that Timothy's faith walk was nominal. They prayed for their son and his family regularly. But they were unaware of the transformation until they received an invitation to attend Yoko's baptism in 2012. A new kind of family unity now encircled the Myer family.

May 2013 was an opportunity for Regina to plan a surprise birthday party for her husband. His sixty-fifth birthday was on a Saturday. Regina drove Cedric toward a restaurant for his celebratory dinner. On the pretense of needing something, she stopped at the church. The parking lot had numerous cars in it. She asked Cedric to retrieve her laptop from the office.

A chorus of "surprise" by a host of friends blindsided him.

Birthday signs and balloons decorated the fellowship hall. Cedric soon discovered that he was to endure a "roast." Friends, co-workers, and a few in the family took their turn telling stories and jokes at his expense. The highlight of the evening came when a slide show started. He tried to identify the narrator and realized it was Dorinda's voice. He believed it was a recorded presentation until he saw her, mic in hand. She showed embarrassing pictures of Cedric's baby to his teen years. Let's say she got even for a lot of brotherly pestering.

It was a birthday he wouldn't forget. It was also a fantastic week after the party, with Dorinda and Mark at the ranch. Mark and Dori planned a trip to Arizona from

Cedric and Regina's home in Masonville to revisit the reservation they had worked at earlier in their marriage.

It seems a little unfair when your child retires before you. Colonel Timothy Myer retired from the USAF in 2015. He had served his country with honor. Now he looked for a way to help his Lord. The relationship with Dr. Paul brought an offer to become Managing Director of Distribution at the Family Ministry. His job was sending tapes, CDs, books, and movies worldwide. And it allowed him to remain in Colorado Springs, his adopted home.

Retirement wasn't seriously on the radar for Cedric in 2015. He did slow some with the number of seminars he conducted. But he liked to work and be active. That hit a snag one Saturday afternoon in August.

"Let's go for a horseback ride up the mountain," Regina suggested.

"I haven't ridden for a couple of months."

"Oh, you'll do alright. It's not that difficult."

"Ok, I'll have Red saddle the horses," Cedric said with reluctance as he got up from his recliner.

They mounted their horses and started up the mountain. Rounding a bend in the trail, a coyote darted from behind a bush. Cedric's horse reared up and threw him onto the ground.

Regina hurried to Cedric's side, who was moaning in pain.

"Don't move. I'll call for help, dear."

The doctor in the emergency room confirmed that Cedric had broken a hip. The pinning, traction, and three-month physical therapy stint made for some long days.

Thank goodness for grandkids who helped Grandpa play lots of table games. Carletta preferred the game, Sorry, and being able to land on other's pawns and send them back to their starting ring. Reggie's interest was more with Uno and making Grandpa draw four as often as possible. Allen learned to play a good game of chess and could usually beat cousin Reggie. But after a few hours of arguing about which game to play or what TV program to watch, Grandpa was ready for some quiet and rest.

Timothy's retirement and the horse accident placed a seed in Cedric's mind. April 16, 2016, was set as the Big "R" day. He wasn't ready to take to the rocker just yet, but the time was right with good health and an adventurous attitude. Cedric and Regina needed to make several advance plans for their bucket list to occur.

First, they sat down with Ruth, Timothy, and their spouses to discuss estate plans. The two children would be named successor trustees of the Revocable Trust. The updating of Cedric and Regina's wills specified the assets' division. They shared copies of each parent's Living Wills and Health Care Representative

Cedric asked Andrew and Ruth to implement an operational plan for the Mount Eden Camp in 2016. Their work included scheduling camps and overseeing accompanying events. Andrew and Ruth were grateful that Barney and Sandy Devinshire became ranch hands a year ago, assisting in Mount Eden's ministry. Cedric would not conduct any seminars that year at the Camp.

The final information shared was Regina and Cedric's post-retirement goal. The purchase of a medium-sized motor home with a tow-behind vehicle would allow them to travel the USA on a year-long trip. With new technology, Zoom would provide face and voice contacts weekly. Cedric and Regina asked permission to let their grandchildren be flown round-trip to Florida during the Christmas period; at Grandpa and Grandma's expense.

At first, the children were not sure how to respond. There were many "what ifs" to consider.

Timothy spoke first, "What if you decide not to come back?"

"The ranch will be yours sooner than anyone planned," Cedric chimed back.

"Are you having a mid-life crisis, dad?" asked Ruth.

"Your dad just wants to complete a bucket list," Regina reassured them.

"Are you dying, Dad?" Tim asked hesitantly.

"I expect to, but not for quite a while."

"Tim and Yoko, we want you to stay at the ranch any time you wish when we are traveling. Ruth might appreciate the support."

"I'm sure Reggie will want to come every week," stated Yoko.

Many days on the computer, mapping out routes, exploring sites to see, setting up schedules to meet friends and family helped prepare for the great adventure. Departure day arrived, June 1, 2016. With Regina and Cedric, the thirty-six-foot Coachman RV with a 2011 Chevy Travers LTZ towed behind left Masonville, Colorado. Both of them had their first Social Security check funds in their billfolds. Ahead of them lay some once-in-a-lifetime experiences. Their shared time together helped buffer their immediate family's separation for such a long time.

The first key destination was Salt Lake City, Utah. The Mormon Tabernacle Choir, with guest Andrea Bocelli, presented an inspirational and moving concert. A day trip west to the Salt Flats was quite a contrast to the Rocky Mountain terrain.

Cedric asked Regina, "How about a dip in Salt Lake to see if you can sink?"

"I think I'm seasoned enough without a salt bath."

Yellowstone National Park, the first national park in the world, was next. A senior National Park pass was secured, allowing entrance anywhere in the USA. Research warned Cedric to make reservations for RV parking, or one might be sleeping fifty miles away. It was preferable to have an inside-the-park hookup with their two-week stay.

"Let's go see Old Faithful spout up," said Regina.

"I agree. Maybe we can do our wash while we're there."

"What do you mean Cedric, there's no laundromat there."

"I heard those old settlers would put their dirty clothes over its opening, and the hot water and steam would do their wash."

As they traveled on the road to the geyser, Cedric spotted a huge herd of bison.

"Don't sneeze, Gina. You might start a stampede."

"We can pretend we are in Dances with Wolves."

"I'll be Kevin Costner," boasted Cedric.

"You wish."

"Maybe tonight you can be Stands With Fist," suggested Cedric.

"I could give you one in your jaw," Regina offered.

The display of Old Faithful was spectacular. They saw contrasting boiling hot pools and almost ice-cold lakes in higher elevations as they traveled through the park. Returning to the motor home for the night, Regina reminded Cedric to put out the trash.

"Be sure to put the garbage in the sealed drums to keep the bears away."

"And you be careful to keep our food tightly contained inside. I don't want an unwelcome visitor barging in for a midnight snack," Cedric replied.

At the Canyon Visitor Education Center the next day, they listened to several interactive recordings.

"It said we are right above one of the biggest pools of molten magma," Cedric noted.

"The volcanologists said it's a matter of time till there will be an eruption," said Regina.

"If there is, over half of the USA would lose crops and get much colder."

"What if it were to explode while we are here?" asked Regina.

"We would have quite a blast."

"Well, we will be going up anyway someday," she said.

Traveling north through "Big Sky Country" displayed both mountains and plains. The goal was Glacier National Park in northwest Montana. The park provided a chance to explore some of the fifty glaciers and 200 pristine lakes. A limited number of roads offered a picturesque view of the park's natural settings. Cedric and Regina were able to take some of the more accessible hiking trails.

July 1 was the aim to arrive at Regina's most desired destination: Calgary, Alberta, Canada.

"I dreamed as a teenager of being at the annual Stampede Rodeo, the granddaddy of all rodeos."

For Regina, it was a chance to go back down memory lane when she was on her Palomino and won the barrel race. As she watched the competition, her heart raced as if she was riding again.

"Do you wish you were down there racing?" Cedric asked teasingly.

"Maybe if I were forty years younger."

"Do you think my queen would beat them?"

"Patsy and I would win by a length."

Going west lay Banff National Park. It ran on either side of the Rocky Mountain ridge. They explored lakes and forests from the town of Banff to the village of Jasper.

"I think Colorado has many grand mountain scenes, but the Canadian Rockies are just awesome," Cedric said.

"I agree, but I'm content with what we've got back home," replied Regina.

Traveling through Vancouver, British Columbia permitted Cedric and Regina to contact their nephew. Dorinda's middle son, Branson, resided there. He graciously took several days off work to show them some sights.

"You'll have to see Stanley Park. We can rent bikes ride along the coast and through the forests," Branson told them.

"Do they have three-wheelers?" asked Cedric.

"I'm not sure, but we can ask. You're not too old for a two-wheeled one, Uncle Cedric."

"I heard there are some totem poles in the park," Regina mentioned.

"Oh yes, Indian art is prolific in our area."

"Do you know much about the tribes that were in the area?" Regina asked.

"Some, but I know a lot more about the Arizona tribes while living with them as a kid."

The first evening Branson introduced them to the Granville Island Market, which contained one of the best seafood restaurants.

"What will it be, Branson, lobster, salmon, or maybe shrimp? I'm buying," promised Cedric.

"Well, in that case, it will be lobster," he replied.

"Make it three lobster tails, waiter," Cedric ordered.

The following day the three of them went to Queen Elizabeth Park. Elevated above the city of Vancouver, it boasts of one of the world's most spectacular gardens.

"The Bloedel Conservatory contains a tropical garden, something unique for us Canadians," said Branson.

"I also read of the Dancing Water Fountain in the park. I'll bet that is quite a display," stated Regina.

"Just don't get caught dancing in the fountain, or you won't get to leave Canada."

"I'll just stick a toe in to test the temperature," Cedric joked.

The time spent with Branson was enjoyed by each one. You could tell he truly appreciated having family take the time to visit him. Cedric and Regina invited him to come to their ranch sometime soon. He said he would consider that.

Crossing into Washington State, they headed for Seattle. The Pike Place Market allowed them to restock their camper's food supply with the most lushes fruits, vegetables, and seafood. One corner fish vendor featured three merchants tossing large whole salmon to one another, standing twenty feet apart. A trip to Seattle was incomplete without a ride to the top of the Space Needle to see a 360-degree view of the town and Puget Sound.

Cedric inquired, "Do you think we could build one of these on the ranch?"

"Maybe if you work twenty-four hours a day for the next hundred years."

The journey on I-5 south allowed them to see the tops of the highest points in Washington, Mt. Rainier at 14,411 feet; Mt. Hood at 11,239 feet east of Portland, Oregon. The motor home objected to climbing both elevations.

A stop at Salem, Oregon, was an opportunity to spend several days with Randy and Kathy Newman. Randy had been a boyhood church friend in Indiana. Spending a Sunday with each other made provision for them to worship together again.

"Randy could you recommend a motor home shop to have an oil change and mechanical look over?" asked Cedric.

"Sure, a good friend of mine has a shop about a mile north of here. We can take it to him Monday," Randy said.

It was now the second month since departing Colorado. The family back home appreciated hearing of Cedric and Regina's adventures. They liked it even better when shown pictures of the places and people they visited. As often as possible, they tried to connect by Zoom when Wi-Fi was available.

With California one of the most extended states to be traveled, Cedric and Regina planned a whole month to pass through it. After a drive along the coastal highway in Oregon, it was back to I-5 south toward Los Angeles. I-5 primarily runs through a valley between the Coastal (west) and Sierra Nevada (east) mountain ranges. This valley produced most of California's crops, including flowers, nuts, vegetables, and grains. Markets along the way were great stops for refreshment and resupply.

Approaching Redding, CA, Cedric thought he heard a vibrating sound. Pulling off at the next exit, he discovered that an inside tire on the dual pair (left rear) had gone flat—Regina Googled for a nearby tire repair facility.

"America's Tires," answered the person on the phone.

"Do you repair motorhome tires?" asked Cedric.

"Sure do, but we close at 6:00 PM. How far away are you?"

"We are three miles from you. We will be there in about fifteen minutes."

"It's 3:30 now. We can get you in by four," the mechanic said.

They were out the door by five, tire repaired, and $100.00 poorer. The best overnight parking place was a Pilot Travel Center truck stop. Besides, they had a Denny's to eat at, which pleased Regina. The next day as they neared Sacramento, a sign informed them, "Reno East on I-80."

"Hey honey, you want to cut over to Reno for a "quickie?" asked Cedric playfully.

Regina responded innocently, "You mean a quick lunch?"

"No, they specialize in quick divorces."

"You want to end this trip here, mister?"

"I think we'll stay on track for San Francisco," Cedric said submissively.

They looked at each other and laughed as they hurried on down the road. Plans were to take a side trip to San Francisco to see some unique sites. China Town, the Golden Gate Bridge was a few. But Cedric had read The Last Guard Out by Jim Albright. The true story of the last correctional officer to leave Alcatraz. A tour of the facility convinced them that a life of crime was not worth spending time there.

The last night in San Francisco, they ate at Fisherman's Warf. Both enjoyed seafood dinners and the Warf's scenic view. In the morning, as they again headed south, Regina said she was feeling a little punky. She had skipped breakfast just drinking some water and sprite. Several hours later, she complained of abdominal pains. Concerned, Cedric started weighing what they should do. Thinking maybe it was the oysters, she took some Tums.

They were coming near Bakersfield, and a sign indicated the exit toward a hospital. Regina entered the Mercy Hospital's Emergency entrance for an examination. Two hours later, she was on the operating table to remove an infected appendix. Fortunately, since it hadn't ruptured, laparoscopic surgery removed it.

"That was a close one. Glad we made it here," noted Cedric.

"They want to keep me overnight."

"That is best for you. I'll find a place nearby to park the RV."

"I should be OK tomorrow," Regina whispered.

"I think we'll stay in Bakersfield for several days to let you rest. You don't need a lot of bouncing around."

Cedric asked Regina upon discharge if she preferred heading back to Colorado. Without hesitation, she determined to continue on their trip.

"I've hurt a lot worse when falling off my horse."

"Well, at least your falls took less time for recovery."

"I'll be fine, my love. Just give me a little time," Regina said.

"We are about three hours from Willow's place."

Cedric contacted Willow about arriving on August 22 at her condo in Burbank. She asked a friend to park the RV inside his secure fenced lot. Willow was excited to have her brother stay at her home and looked forward to showing them the town. She took them to see Hollywood's walk of fame, the home locations of a few well-known stars. They completed the day with window shopping at a few Rodeo Drive stores.

When asked how her dance studio was going and if she had any contracts as a choreographer, she said it was better than expected.

"I am currently waiting to hear from Disney Studios for my proposal to provide dancers in an upcoming movie."

"Do let us know if you get the nod. I want to see your name on the big screen."

Regina added, "How many clients do you have taking lessons?"

"About eighty in three different levels of classes."

When the week was over, Willow hugged her brother and thanked him for taking the time to come her way.

"You don't know how much this means to me to have you come to see me," Willow said.

"You know that you can come to the ranch any time you want a break from LA congestion," Cedric offered.

Goodbyes said; Cedric and Regina hit the road. On September 1, the RV pulled into Lake Mead's Park. Las Vegas, also known as "Sin City," was a few miles to the west. Here gambling and divorce are legally offered. Prostitution is obtainable, both legally and illegally.

Cedric and Regina drove down the Vegas Strip to see all the lights and rowdy crowds packing the sidewalks the first night in Las Vegas. While there, they got tickets to see Donnie and Marie. The second show they watched was an Elvis review with acrobatic performers doing phenomenal acts. Regina and Cedric spent the last day touring Hoover Dam, which held Lake Mead and the Colorado River.

No road safe for RV's goes directly east from Las Vegas to the Grand Canyon. So it meant going south on Arizona-93, to I-40 east, then north on Arizona-64. This canyon of all canyons was genuinely grand in size and formation. To imagine water's power cutting a hole this deep and wide was nearly illogical. Perhaps there may have been a little divine help. Six days camping there was time well spent.

The next stop would be the second-longest stay of the trip. Mark and Dorinda would be meeting Regina and Cedric for a four-week camp at Holbrook, AZ. The Petrified Forest National Park was nearby. But the main draw was the Apache, Navajo, and Hopi reservations, which were north and south of Holbrook. Mark and Dorinda had worked with the Hopi Tribe in their early married days. Now they annually returned for several months to continue work with the tribe.

Several opportunities let Cedric and Regina join Dori and Mark to help them. The tribal council gave consent for their presence and welcomed the assistance. The project this year was constructing a new school structure.

The time spent with Mark and Dorinda showed evidence that age may be catching up with them. Mark was constantly losing his keys. Dorinda had some lapses in recalling names. But the most obvious was their hearing loss. Regina and Cedric just tried not to laugh.

"Where did you put the checkbook?" asked Dori.

"I never touched your checkered boot," was Mark's reply.

"I don't have a chest of loot," Dori responded.

"You know, Dori, I think we need to learn sign language."

But all kidding aside, they had a good time talking of the past, family, and faith. Politics were best left unspoken. The four played many games of Euchre and Dominos. The guys won most card games, but the girls beat the snot out of the guys with the "bones" (dominos). Cedric liked to rub in his sister's mistakes in Euchre, especially when she failed to follow suit. Dorinda, of course, had to try getting in another zinger on her brother.

"Remember this," she said, holding up her left hand.

"I refuse to accept any guilt for that; you grabbed the muzzle," Cedric stated.

"Yes, but you pulled the trigger."

By 1957, the major east-west road through New Mexico was Route 66. I-40 replaced it but often skirted small towns in its path. This road became the slow death for much of the nostalgic tourist attractions of the earlier years of the twentieth century.

Tucumcari, once known as "Ragtown," and later, Six Shooter Siding," was one of those towns near the east end of New Mexico. Cedric and Regina found old motels, cafes, and museums trying to capture the lure of foregone days.

No trip was complete through the Texas panhandle without a stop at Amarillo's Big Texan Steakhouse. Cedric planned to take up the restaurant's challenge for a free steak. One only had to eat a seventy-two-ounce steak along with potato, beans, salad, and dinner roll in one hour. Of those who tried it, only about ten percent were successful. The ninety percent who weren't able had to pay the hefty price for a seventy-two-ounce steak dinner.

Regina warned Cedric, "You're going to be sorry."

Ignoring her warning and some voice in his head about avoiding gluttony, he started to eat. A waiter noted that a lady held the record to date, finishing the meal in eight minutes. Inhaling four and one-half pounds of beef didn't sound like a good strategy. Cedric planned to pace himself and alternate between food items. Eight minutes in, he felt relatively comfortable. But Mr. Myer had about three pounds of meat left. He was beginning to sweat with thirty minutes to go and had doubts.

People will do some crazy things to get their name in lights. Bragging rights can appeal to others seeking notoriety. Cedric realized that neither of these was worth the misery he faced for accomplishing the feat. The hour timer went off, a large rib eye-sized steak looked back at him, and he owed the total price for the effort.

Regina laughed, "I told you," as he made his fourth trip to the bathroom that night.

Breakfast the following day consisted of two eggs, bacon, hash browns with orange juice, all eaten by Regina. Cedric had a cup of coffee. The moral he took from this was, "a steer in the field is more desirable than one in your gut." He tried to imagine how the eight-minute lady felt the day after.

There were several reasons for the Myers to stop in the Dallas, Texas, area on this trip. One was to watch a preseason game between the Denver Broncos and Dallas Cowboys. Secondly, Cedric had heard a lot about Dallas Theological Seminary and desired to tour it. But the primary purpose was to attend the church where Dr. Jack Hammer was senior pastor.

The Broncos won the football game to the delight of Cedric and Regina. AT&T Stadium was quite phenomenal in size and design.

"You know Regina, the Cowboy Cheerleaders add a good atmosphere to the game."

"Just watch the game, Mr. google eyes," warned Regina.

Sunday's worship service was very inspirational, with the powerful preaching of Dr. Jack Hammer. He made the Scriptures come to life and provided practical response suggestions from it. A visit on Tuesday to the seminary offered an excellent affirmation of its sound reputation. A bonus part of that visit was crossing the path of Dr. Hammer.

"Howdy, folks. What brings you to Dallas?"

"We came to see and hear you. We were in the second service last Sunday," replied Cedric.

"Did you enjoy the worship experience?"

"Very much so, and I listen to you often on the radio. The first time I heard you, you preached at our church in Fort Collins, Colorado, in 1977."

"My," Dr. Hammer noted, "that was a while ago. I hope I've improved since then."

"Your challenge then is why I committed to serve the Lord in family ministry the last thirty-plus years. Perhaps just as important," continued Cedric, "your videotape titled "The Grace In Forgiveness" spurred me to a renewed relationship with Christ and saved our marriage. I want to thank you."

Cedric shared more about how the Lord had used him and Regina in the Fort Collins area.

Dr. Hammer placed his hand on both of them and prayed for God's blessing and protection on their remaining trip. They considered this encounter to be one of the most important in their travels.

Regina and Cedric decided to go through New Orleans on their way to Alabama. The Cajun cuisine was a new style of eating for them to try.

"Regina, you ought to try making Jambalaya and Gumbo when we get home."

"Mine might not taste as good, but I think I could make one of these Bananas Fosters for you. You won't dare to drink the rest of the rum," said Regina.

They visited a museum that detailed the devastation the city had suffered when Hurricane Katrina hit. They both decided that they were glad to live in Colorado. Snowstorms are less destructive than hurricanes.

They arrived in Gulf Shores at the end of October and made it their home until November. While their park was several blocks off the Gulf, they quickly became regular beachcombers. Little by little, their lily-white skin became tanned. Regina and Cedric initiated a friendship with people from about every state in Union. It was in the tourist off-season. Neither the streets nor beaches were crowded like in the Spring and Summer.

Cedric and Regina shook the sand out of their shoes, shorts, and the RV to head for a twelve-week exploration of Florida. They stopped on the way through Pensacola at the Naval Air Museum. It displayed an excellent aviation history of the US Navy and the home of the Navy Thunderbirds.

"Timothy might enjoy seeing this place. I presume the Navy would let an Air Force veteran in," said Cedric

"It's hard to imagine how our flyboys survived in many of these machines," added Regina.

Cedric and Regina set up the RV at different locations for one week to maximize their exposure to Florida's various aspects. At Gainesville, they were in the heart of orange groves. From Ft. Myers, a ferry shipped them to Key West for a day trip.

The drive to Ft. Lauderdale took them through the Everglades on Alligator Alley (I-75).

They stopped at an oasis in the Everglades. "Check the stool carefully in the bathroom, Regina; there are thousands of pythons loose."

"I think I'll just use the motorhome's toilet." While parked near Merritt Island, they could see a night rocket launch from Cape Canaveral.

"Now that's some fireworks display," commented Regina.

"I'll book the next moon trip for you," Cedric offered.

"No thanks, I can see the moon well enough from the ground."

But the best part of their Florida stay was having their grandchildren with them for nearly a week. Carletta, Reginald, and Allen arrived at the Orlando International Airport on December 26. The direct flight from Denver gave parents and grandparents a secure feeling.

Grandma asked, "Tell me what you liked best about the jet ride."

"I liked having my movie screen. I watched "Frozen," Carletta piped in.

From Reginald, "The best part for me was the takeoff and sitting at a window."

"My favorite was the stewardess," Allen said sheepishly.

"Are you all hungry? We'll take you to get pizza."

"Yes. All we had on the plane was peanuts and a cookie."

Cedric had made reservations at a motel near Universal Studios. A suite with two Queen beds and an extra roll-away provided satisfactory sleeping arrangements. Tickets had been purchased for two days at Disney World and one day at Universal. The kids enjoyed the various rides but disliked waiting in lines repeatedly. The family spent hours at the motel pool and arcade machines. The time devoted together became an invaluable bonding time for all. These six days were one of the best Christmas gifts for the Myers.

On New Year's Day, the three amigos were boarded on a 10 AM flight back to Denver. Kisses all around were a send-off with promises to see one another in May. Ruth called her mom to inform her after the kids were safely on the ground in Denver.

Regina and Cedric reminisced about the wonderful time everyone had.

"This was such a special time for us, and I hope the kids," said Regina.

Cedric added, "It sure was. They are growing up so fast."

"They'll be adults tomorrow."

"I guess we better hurry home before that happens."

The grandkids with them for a week suddenly gave Cedric and Regina a little homesickness. Were it not for the weekly Zoom connections, they might have considered cutting the trip short and headed for Colorado. But they also looked forward to seeing parts of the country not yet visited.

Upon leaving Jacksonville on February 26, they traveled up I-95. Cedric stopped several days in Georgia, both Carolinas and Virginia. A week's stay near Washington DC allowed them to visit Arlington Cemetery, the many memorials in the Mall, some Smithsonian Museums, and the Capital Building. A renewed sense of patriotism was the takeaway.

The next major city to visit was New York. Large cities are not the friendliest for a motorhome to travel, especially during the rush hours. Once parked in a nearby RV park, the Travers became the commute vehicle into the inner cities. In some cases, the train system was the most convenient transportation means. In addition to the Empire State Building, Regina wished to see a Broadway production of the "Phantom of the Opera."

Because of weather and wanting to reduce some miles, a change of plans led Cedric to divert and go from NYC through Pennsylvania's center on I-80. Being March, the prospect of getting snow was relatively high. Not intending to be a prophet, as they neared Clarion, PA, a giant storm dumped ten inches of snow, stranding them for three days. They were fortunate to find a motel vacancy in a warmer room.

"This RV's design isn't for driving in this kind of weather," said Cedric.

"The heater isn't quite keeping up either," noted Regina.

"I'm sure glad we made it to the exit before they shut the interstate down."

When the roads cleared, Cedric and Regina continued the journey west. The temperatures had moderated and were in the mid-sixties in the afternoon. They headed for the Holmes County area of Ohio to visit the Amish communities. Cedric's ancestors had migrated to Indiana from this region. When Regina got an up-close look into an Amish horse and buggy, she was intrigued.

"Now that's a horse of a different order."

"I don't think you would ride any of them in a barrel race."

"I bet you I could train one to race."

"You would have to talk differently. Those horses only understand German," said Cedric.

Cedric explained to Regina some of the Amish people's traditions and culture. She liked the idea of a simple lifestyle but wasn't ready to adopt their dress. A stop at an Amish furniture store made her prepared to transport a new dining room table in the RV. Cedric suggested having one shipped by Amazon.

By the first part of April, they were back in Cedric's boyhood hometown. Willis and Candice had asked them to stay at their house. Willis's children had all moved from the home, providing plenty of bedroom space.

"Could I get you to service the RV for me?"

"Of course," said Willis. "The business has been a little slow lately."

"You might want to check the coolant. The gage has been running hot."

"We'll give her the A-1 treatment."

Willis discovered that the thermostat was faulty and needed replacing. Willis also suggested that Cedric might want to visit Bob. He had heard that Bob was not well but didn't know why. Cedric drove the tow car to Bob's home. Bob appeared ashen and thin.

"Hello, friend. Willis told me you're not feeling well."

"No, I'm not. Two months ago, I was diagnosed with pancreatic cancer."

"I'm so sorry, Bob. What are they giving you for treatment?"

"They just gave me pain meds. I was at stage five when they found it.:

"What are they saying about time."

"I may have another month or two at the most."

"How's Monica dealing with it?"

"She's angry and scared.

"Are you ready to die? Are you at peace with God?"

"It took me a few weeks, but I know where I'm going."

"Someday, we'll be friends there together," noted Cedric confidently.

Leaving Bob was difficult, knowing it was likely their last time together on earth. Cedric promised Bob to stay in close contact and asked him to call at any hour. He would also seek God's mercy for him through the process.

"Even though I walk through the valley of the shadow of death, I will fear no evil, for you are with me, your rod and your staff, they comfort me." Psalm 23:4

Cedric asked Willis to keep Cedric informed of Bob's progress. When the time came, and Bob was gone, Cedric asked Willis and Candice to reach out to Monica to comfort and offer help with life. To both these requests, Willis promised his assistance. Cedric knew he could depend on Willis to be a "determined protector"(his name meaning) of the weak and helpless.

Rowena and Brad still lived in Naperville, IL. A call to verify their availability for a visit settled the plan to drop by. Rowena asked Cedric and Regina to stay for a couple of days. Brad had requested downtime and would also be home. The two couples spent the time catching up on family information, taking walks around town, and eating at local restaurants. All except Rowena were a bit travel weary.

Cedric and Regina conversed about further excursions. They considered going to South Dakota to look at the Bad Lands and Mt. Rushmore. But home was calling them to come. So they headed directly from Nussbaum's on I-80 for Masonville, CO.

On the three-day drive through Illinois, Iowa, and Nebraska, they reviewed all they had experienced and places they had seen. Despite flat tires, surgeries, and sad news, the trip was worth it. As a couple, they were more in sync than ever. They hadn't grown tired of each other's company. Regina and Cedric's love had grown deeper during the last twelve months. Their marriage required maintenance too.

CHAPTER 8

Winterizing

Being home in your bed brings great relaxation and, ultimately, sleep. As Cedric lay there, he thought of his family and how dear each was. Then he heard a noise outside. One of the horses neighed once, twice, then three times. A calf let out a loud cry, with a battering of the stalls about the exact moment.

Cedric got up, threw on pants and a jacket, grabbed a flashlight, and ran to the barn. Several horses now were bellowing. He flung the door open and entered. The main commotion was coming from the back part of the barn at the calf pens. As Cedric approached, his light flashed on a horrific scene. A large mountain lion had clamped its teeth on the throat of a baby calf, preparing to drag it outside.

Not quite sure what to do, Cedric let out a yell hoping to chase the lion away. Instead, this predator looked at Cedric with penetrating eyes. The lion let loose of the calf, jumped over the fence, and began stalking toward Cedric. There was no defensive tool to grab, and he knew running would encourage the lion to chase him.

In fear, Cedric again gave a loud command. The lion kept coming toward him. At that moment, Cedric realized that it was a lost cause. Death was imminent. He turned and began running, screaming at the top of his lungs and flailing his arms. And then it had him; he felt the sharp teeth sink into his arms, knocking him down.

"Cedric, Cedric, wake up," cried Regina as she gripped his swinging arm, sinking her sharp nails into it.

Cedric woke with a start. Sweat drenched his body, and his heart was palpitating wildly. Breathlessly he related to Regina the scary details of what he had dreamt. It was so real, and he thought sure he would die.

"In the last days, God says, 'I will pour out my Spirit on all people. Your sons and daughters will prophesy, your young men will see visions, your old men will dream dreams." Acts 2:17

Cedric noticed that his dreams were more frequent and disturbing since approaching seventy. Some were bizarre, others nonsensical, and a few slightly risqué. Mixed in with these were the pleasant dreams and of comforting material, often dealing with family.

There have been many theories of the source of dreams. A few believe they stem from life experiences or thought patterns just before sleep. Others have suggested a drug can affect nightmares. And some just attribute them to a wrong dietary choice.

Dreams almost always have an emotional component to them. Fear, anxiety, anger, and love can influence the dream's direction. Upon waking, one will account for the emotional feeling quicker than details about the vision.

But a mystery for scientists, psychologists, and spiritualists is the meaning of dreams. The answer is not definitive. Some hold a theory that they are simply the result of random brain activity. Others believe that they may predict future events.

Cedric searched for some meaning in the mountain lion dream. He knew that he was in the latter days of his life. Was it such a reminder? But he knew that Acts 2:17 was a reference to a period in God's economy for all post-Pentecost saints. Maybe it was God's way of saying, "you're in the category of old men," and therefore prone to dream. But again, the 2:17 dreams were specific means of God's Spirit to speak to a person.

Cedric hoped it wasn't a prediction of his imminent demise or method. He was at peace about his eventual death, having prepared with God and those who would take over his affairs. But death by a mountain lion was not a preferred way to go.

At breakfast the following day, Regina and Cedric discussed the dream experience.

"You scared me with your yelling and swinging."

"Gina, it was so real. I thought I was a goner."

"I noticed you've been quite restless the last while. Maybe you should see a doctor."

"What kind of doctor? A GP or a Psych?"

"Why don't you start with Dr. Proboski? He knows you best."

Dr. Proboski went through the routine exam for "old men" and asked a series of questions. He didn't think a psychiatrist was the appropriate next step. Instead, he set up an appointment to do a sleep study. It required an overnight test at a clinic. Cedric complied and did the test.

A sleep apnea machine became a new resident in the Myers bedroom. It took some adjustment for both, but Cedric began sleeping better at night in time. He convinced himself that the mask was like being an AF jet pilot. The increased REM sleep allowed for the potential of more dreams. Thankfully there were fewer disturbing ones.

Cedric had continued offering more marriage seminars and retreats after returning from the RV trip. He had shifted to a focus for marriages thirty-five to sixty years in duration. He had noticed that there was an increasing number of marriages dissolving in this age grouping. Surprisingly, this bunch was a little more resistant to seeking help. Cedric was able to identify with this crowd due to his age and marital experiences.

Regina and Cedric's fiftieth wedding anniversary was more sedate than the twenty-fifth. Regina preferred a meal with the immediate family at the Lamplighter plus a weekend at a Denver hotel. They were no less passionate, just enjoying the more simple lifestyle. Cedric ordered an extendable oak dining room table with chairs from an Amish craftsman in Holmes County, Ohio, for Regina.

Carletta Reese married her high school boyfriend a month after Regina and Cedric's Golden Anniversary, which blessed the Myer family. And on Cedric's seventy-fifth birthday, Carletta gave birth to a baby boy. They saddled the poor guy with the name Cedric Ryan. Great-grandpa had a button-bursting celebration.

> *"The length of our days is seventy years—or eighty if we have the strength; yet their span is but trouble and sorrow, for they quickly pass, and we fly away."* Psalm 90:10

Wintertime of life can be a beautiful experience, like a gentle flurry that clings to tree limbs and blankets the ground. On the other hand, old age can cause an avalanche of disease, accidents, and disabilities. The latter is the case for Cedric's siblings.

Mark Threadgood called Cedric on August 10, 2015.

"I wanted to let you know that Dorinda is in the hospital."

"What happened to her?" asked Cedric.

On our last day on the reservation a week ago, a venomous spider bit her on her leg. She developed over 104 degrees temperature for five days," said Mark.

"So, what is the prognosis?"

"Her brain has swollen, and she's developed Alopecia.

Dorinda remained in the hospital for six weeks before going home. Recovery took several months before she was back to normal. Mark did his best to give her the care she needed.

Rowena's situation became equally sad. On Christmas Day of 2017, Brad's airplane crashed landed in Istanbul, Turkey. There were no survivors. Rowena then married

Samuel Oyster, a Chicago real estate tycoon, on October 17, 2020. They moved into a downtown penthouse in Chicago.

Rowena attended gallant social affairs with Sam's daughter, Pearl Oyster. Rowena relished the lifestyle of Parada suits, Gucci shoes, and Vera Wang purses.

Cedric contacted Willis by phone. The brothers discussed the situations involving the two older sisters.

"Tell me, Willis, are you doing OK?"

"Well, not really. I went to the doctor last month and was diagnosed with Planters Warts."

"Did they remove it?" asked Cedric

"The problem is that there are at least six on the heels of each foot. And the specialist believes more will continue to surface indefinitely."

"How are you treating them? Can you even walk?" inquired Cedric.

"No, I can't walk because it is excruciatingly painful." Willis added, "My only relief is to soak my feet in hot Carter's Peanut Oil that I get from Americus, Georgia."

"Who is running the shop?" asked Cedric.

"I've had to close it. I may need to sell it to pay medical expenses. We don't have medical insurance."

Cedric tried to encourage his brother but found few words that were all that beneficial. Then Willis gave him some more bad news.

"By the way, Cedric, have you heard that Mark is now in a convalescent home?

"Why, what happened to him?"

"He was found to have a very aggressive form of Alzheimer's."

"My O my. Does it never end?" Cedric replied.

"Dorinda struggled with admitting him, but she just couldn't handle him anymore. Mark began getting quite violent."

"Have her boys given her any help?" asked Cedric.

"I guess Branson moved back in with his mom to help her."

Well, it didn't end with that bit of news. In March of 2021, a significant fault shifted in California, causing a 9.5 Richter scale earthquake. Most high-rise buildings in Los Angeles collapsed, including Catalina Towers, where Willow lived. A confirmation followed that she was in her condo and did not survive.

If there was any redeeming outcome, it was Willow's final written requests. Her attorney revealed that her net worth was more than 1.5 million dollars. She gave one-half of her estate to fund student scholarships to train ballerinas at Julliard. The balance of the estate went to Cedric, whom she adored and trusted. She believed Cedric would use the money wisely.

Cedric did use Willow's money to help both Dorinda and Willis with their mounting medical bills. Numerous charities also benefited from her funds.

Cedric and Regina compared the Winter of their life to his siblings. They were very fortunate and divinely blessed. How Cedric wished he could intervene and change his sibling's circumstances. The only thing left to do was treasure their past lives and be available to them when needed.

Age had taken its toll on Regina and Cedric. By their mid-seventies, Regina's hair was a beautiful snow-white. At least she had some. Cedric's head was more like a billiard ball. Arthritis had set into Cedric's broken hip area, and Regina had a lumpectomy as a precaution.

But despite a few bumps in the road, both Regina and Cedric could say life was much more gratifying and joyous than trouble and sorrow. Looking back at this venture, it did seem like the years had gone by rapidly. But they thankfully made the most of them. Neither would have wished for a Methuselah span of 969 years.

With the end of life not that far ahead, Cedric and Regina mulled over some questions. Just how long will they live? What will the quality of life be at the end? How many more great-grandchildren will there be? What kind of world will the progeny's face.

"If I die first, would you marry again?" Regina mused.

"Yes, if I can find a Regina clone."

"Just make sure she can barrel race."

"That'll mean she would be under twenty-five."

"You'd probably have a heart attack keeping up with her."

"You're more my speed, baby."

"We've had a great trail ride together," replied Regina.

Epilogue

Cedric did not simply walk off the end of the trail of life into oblivion. His earthly existence was the prelude to his future body. He was an eternal being.

Through Jesus Christ (Son of God) providing his life as the payment for man's imperfection (sin), Cedric had an avenue to eternal life. He simply needed to accept the Savior's sacrifice by faith. No personal merit was adequate to gain admission. [Ephesians 2:8-9; Revelation 21:27]

Cedric would no longer operate under the mandates of chronological time. Hours, days, and years will not be one's measurement. Eternity is time without end.

This eternal life promised him many things:

A new home built by God [John 14:2]

A new city with indescribable splendor [Revelation 21]

A new indestructible body [2 Corinthians 5:1; Luke 20:36]

A new heaven and earth [2 Peter 3:13]

This life is equally glorious for what is missing:

No hunger, thirst, or scorching sun [Revelation 7:16]

No sorrow, pain or tears [Revelation 7:17; 21:4]

No evil influences [Revelation 20:10; 21:27]

For Cedric and all who like him have made reservations, there awaits this beautiful life. The most desirable part is to be with God, never to be separated again. Cedric invites you to join him.

Made in the USA
Columbia, SC
13 June 2022

61650714R00057